8

2

LEA

"What are we going to do?" he asked at last.

Emily pushed away from him and walked over to the window. He knew the view she was afforded from the window. This place had been hard-earned. He'd worked just as hard as his siblings to make Montoro Enterprises into the success it was today.

"I just wanted you to know. Beyond that I don't need anything. Someday the kid is going to ask about you—"

"Someday? I'm going to be a part of this," Rafe said.

"I don't see how. You're going to be jetting off to Alma to take the throne. My life is here. The baby's life will be here."

He rubbed the back of his neck. The timing on this sucked. But he didn't blame Emily. He'd been running when he went to Key West, afraid to admit that he was in over his head. He was the oldest son. He was Rafael the Fourth, the future king. He should be in command all the time. But the truth was he was lost.

And somehow in Emily's arms he'd found something.

Carrying
a King's Child

KATHERINE
GARBERA

MILLS
BOON

First published in Great Britain 2015
by Mills & Boon, an imprint of Harlequin (UK) Limited,
Large Print edition 2015
Eton House, 18-24 Paradise Road,
Richmond, Surrey, TW9 1SR

© 2015 Harlequin Books S.A.

ISBN: 978-0-263-26038-0

Special thanks and acknowledgement are given to Katherine Garbera for her contribution to the *Dynasties: The Montoros* miniseries.

Harlequin (UK) Limited's policy is to use papers that are natural, renewable and recyclable products and made from wood grown in sustainable forests. The logging and manufacturing processes conform to the legal environmental regulations of the country of origin.

Printed and bound in Great Britain
by CPI Antony Rowe, Chippenham, Wiltshire

KATHERINE GARBERA

is a *USA TODAY* bestselling author of more than fifty books and has always believed in happy endings. She lives in England with her husband, children and their pampered pet, Godiva. Visit Katherine on the web at katherinegarbera.com, or catch up with her on Facebook and Twitter.

This book is for my Facebook posse
who are always willing to
chat about hot guys, good reads
and the general craziness of life.

One

Emily Fielding was shaking as she stepped off the elevator into the foyer of Rafael Montoro IV's penthouse in South Beach. The Montoros had settled in Miami, Florida, decades ago, when as the royal family of Alma, they had to flee their European island homeland because of a coup. Now the dictator who'd replaced them was dead and the parliament of Alma wanted the Montoros back.

With Rafe as king.

Great. Happy ending for everyone. Well, everyone except for Emily, the bartender who was pregnant with the soon-to-be-king's baby.

Or at least that was what her gut told her. Her gut and three home pregnancy tests. She wasn't easy to convince.

She had debated not telling Rafe about the baby, but having grown up without knowing who her father was, she just couldn't do that to her own child. Sure, she'd had to lie to get up here to his very posh penthouse apartment, and she knew her timing sucked because Rafe had a lot of royal duties to attend to before his coronation, but she was still here.

Getting past security hadn't been that easy, but she'd made a few calls to friends and found that one of them had a connection to Rafe via a maid service. So she'd used Maria's pass to get into the gated community and her key to get into his building.

Sneaking around wasn't her style. Normally. But nothing about this situation was normal.

She was shaking as she stood on the Italian marble floor and let the air-conditioning dry the sweat at the small of her back. Luxurious and well appointed, the apartment was exactly the sort of place where she expected to find Rafe. His family might have fled Alma in the middle of the night, but they'd brought their dignity and their determination with them to the United States and this generation of Montoros had truly flourished.

Rafe was the CEO of Montoro Enterprises. He had been featured in *Forbes* long before the recent developments in Alma. He'd earned the wealth she saw around him, and the fact that he played as hard as he worked was something she could respect. She played hard, too.

She forced herself not to touch her stomach. Not to draw attention to the one thing that changed everything. Since she'd looked at that stick in the bathroom and realized she was going to have a baby, everything had changed.

Pretending that there was more to her visit than ensuring that her child would know who its father was would be stupid. A wealthy businessman she could have had a shot with, she thought. But not a king.

Still…

She'd seen photos of Alma. With its white sand beaches and castle that looked like something out of a dream, it was a beautiful place. The kind of place that she might have dreamed about as a little girl. A fairy-tale kingdom with a returning prince. Sounded perfect, right?

Except that Rafael Montoro IV was a playboy and they'd had a fling. She wrinkled her nose as she tried to come up with something else to call it, but a two-night stand didn't cover it, either. One weekend spent in each other's arms. She could lose herself in the memories if she wasn't careful.

Hell, she hadn't been careful. Which was precisely why she was here. Pregnant and determined. She walked down the hallway toward the sounds of Jay-Z playing in the distance. She paused in the doorway of his bedroom.

She'd had to charm her way upstairs, but no way could this wait another moment. Rafe needed to know before he left. She needed to tell him.

She felt queasy and swallowed hard.

There were right and wrong ways to deliver this news, and as appealing to her sense of outrage as it would be to throw up on his carpet, she was hoping for a little sophistication. Just a tiny bit.

After all, she'd seen pictures of his sister and jet-setting mother, though his mother wasn't really in the picture since her divorce from Rafe III. Still she was an elegant woman.

She cleared her throat.

She listened to Jay-Z and Kanye West singing about how there's no church in the wild. She almost laughed out loud as she watched Rafe stop packing his suitcase and start to rap along. She leaned against the doorjamb and admitted her anger was really fear. She wasn't mad at him. She just wanted him to be a different kind of guy so that she could have the fairy tale she wanted.

Not a castle and a title, but a man who loved her. A man who wanted to share his life with her and raise children by her side.

And no matter how fun Rafe was, his path lay

somewhere else. He was duty-bound to become the constitutional monarch of Alma. She was determined to return to Key West and live out her life. She wasn't interested in being involved with a royal; besides, she'd read in the papers that the heirs would have to marry people with spotless reputations.

He was really getting into dancing around the room and rapping.

She applauded when he finished and he turned to look at her.

"What are you doing here?" he asked, shock apparent on his face.

His body was tense. She suspected he was a tiny bit embarrassed to be caught rapping. Nerves made her mouthy. She knew that. So she should just say she was sorry for using her friend's key to get into his penthouse.

But that wasn't her way.

"Hello to you, too, Your Majesty. Should I curtsy or something? I'm not sure of the rules."

"Neither am I," he admitted. "Juan Carlos

doesn't like it when I am seen doing something…well, so American but also undignified."

"Your secret is safe with me," she said. "Who is Juan Carlos?"

"Juan Carlos Salazar II, my cousin, head of the Montoro Family Trust and advocate of decorum at all times."

"He sounds like a stuffed shirt," she said. "I doubt I'd meet with his approval."

"Emily, what are you doing here? And how did you get up here? Security is usually very hard to get past."

"I have my ways."

"And they are?" he asked.

"My charm," she said.

He shook his head. "I'm going to have to warn them about feisty redheads."

"I actually used a key that I procured from your maid service."

"You've been reduced to criminal behavior. Curiouser and curiouser. Why are you here? Did you decide that you wanted to give me a proper send-off?" he asked. He strode over to her, his big body moving with an economy of motion that captivated her. The same way it had when she'd first glimpsed him in the crowded Key West bar where she worked as a bartender.

He was tall—well over six feet—and muscly, but he moved with grace and she could honestly watch him all day long.

"Why are you here, Red? You said goodbye was forever."

Goodbye.

She'd meant it when he'd left. He was a rich guy from Miami and experience had shown her they were only in Key West for one thing. Having given it to him she'd wanted to ensure she didn't give into temptation a second time.

"I did mean it."

"Help me, Red. I don't want to jump to conclusions," he said.

She chewed her lower lip. Up close she could see the flecks of green in his hazel eyes.

He was easily one of the most attractive men she'd ever seen. He'd make a killing in Hollywood with those thick eyelashes and those cheekbones. It wouldn't matter if he could act, just putting him on screen would draw the masses in.

She wished she were immune.

"I'm pregnant."

He stumbled backward and looked at her as if she'd just started speaking in tongues.

Pregnant!

He stepped back and walked over to the Bose speaker on the dresser to turn off the music. A baby. From what he knew of the tough-as-nails-bartender, he could guess she wouldn't be standing in his penthouse apartment if he wasn't the father. His first reaction was joy.

A child.

It wasn't something he'd ever thought he wanted. He hardly knew Emily so had no idea if she was here for money or something else. But knowing his child was growing inside of her stirred something primal. Something very powerful. The baby was his.

Maybe that was just because it gave him

something to think about other than the recent decision that had been made for him.

He'd been dreading his trip to Alma. He was flattered that the country that had once driven his family out had come back to them and asked him to be the next king, but he had grown up here in Florida. He didn't want to be a stuffy royal.

He didn't want European paparazzi following him around and trying to catch him doing anything that would bring shame to his family. God, knew he worked and played hard.

"Rafe?"

"Yeah?"

"Did you hear what I said?" Emily asked.

He had. A baby. Lord knew his father hadn't been the best and as a result, Rafe had thought he'd never have kids. It wasn't as if either of his parents had set a great example. And he was still young, but damn if he wasn't feeling much older every day.

"Yeah, I did. Are you sure?" he asked at last.

She gave him a fiery look from those aqua-blue eyes of hers. He'd seen the passionate side of her nature, and he guessed he was about to witness her temper. "Would I be here if I wasn't?"

He held his hand up.

"Slow down, Red. I didn't mean are you sure it's mine. I meant…are you sure you're pregnant?"

"Damned straight."

"I get it. I had to take three at-home pregnancy tests and visit the doctor before I believed it myself. But trust me, Rafe. I'm positive I'm pregnant and that the baby is yours."

"This is a little surreal," he said.

"I know," she said, with just a hint of softening on in her tone. "Listen, I know you can't turn your back on your family and marry me and frankly, we only had one weekend together so I'd have to say no. But…I don't want this kid to grow up without any knowledge of you."

"Me either."

She glanced up, surprised.

To be honest, he sort of surprised himself. But

he knew all the things not to do as a dad thanks to his own father. It didn't seem right for a kid of his to grow up without him. He wanted that. If he had a child, he wanted a chance to share the Montoro legacy…not the one newly sprung on him that came with a throne, but the one he'd carved out for himself in business. "Don't look shocked."

"You've kind of got a lot going on right now. And having a kid with me isn't going to go over well."

"Tough," he said. He still wasn't sure he wanted to be king of Alma. He and his siblings hadn't grown up with the attitude that they were royalty. They were regular American kids who'd never expected to go back to Alma. "I still make my own decisions."

"I know that," she said. She tucked a strand of hair behind her ear. "I've just been so crazy since I realized I was pregnant and alone. I didn't know what to do. You know my mom raised me by herself…"

He closed the gap between them again and

pulled her into his arms. He hadn't realized she'd been raised by a single parent. To be honest, a weekend of hot sex didn't really lend itself to sharing each other's past like that. "You're not by yourself."

She looked up at him. That little pointed nose of hers was the tiniest bit red and her lip quivered as if she were struggling to keep from crying. That's when he realized how out of character it was for Emily to be unsure. The baby—his baby—had thrown her for a loop as well.

"Thanks. I just need…I have no idea. I mean, a kid. I never expected this. But we used protection."

"I didn't the third time, remember? I was out and we…"

She blushed and rested her forehead against the middle of his chest, wrapped her arms around his waist and held him. He'd thought he hated being trapped, but in Emily's arms this didn't feel constricting.

"Ugh. My mom was right."

"About what?" he asked. He looked over her head at the man in the mirror and remembered how many times he'd wanted to see some substance reflected back. Was this it? Of course it was. The baby would change things. He had no idea how or why, but he knew this moment was going to be the one that helped forge his future and the man he'd become.

"She said all it takes is a sweet-talking man and one time to get pregnant."

"I'm a sweet-talking man?" He tipped her head up with his finger under her chin.

"You can be."

"What are we going to do?" he asked at last. It was clear she'd run out of steam as soon as she entered the room. Marriage was the noble thing to do. He knew that's what Juan Carlos would suggest, but he and Emily were strangers, and tying their lives together didn't seem smart until they knew each other better.

She pushed away from him and walked over to the window. He knew the view she was afforded. This place had been hard-earned. He'd worked just as his siblings had to make Montoro Enterprises into the success it was today.

"I just wanted you to know. Beyond that I don't need anything. Someday the kid is going to ask about you—"

"Someday? I'm going to be a part of this," Rafe said.

"I don't see how. You're going to be jetting off to Alma to take the throne. My life is here. The baby's life will be here."

He rubbed the back of his neck. The timing on this sucked. But he didn't blame Emily. He'd been running when he went to Key West, afraid to admit that he was in over his head. He'd just gotten word that his family was definitely interested in returning to Alma and as the oldest son he was expected to take the throne.

He was the oldest son. He was Rafael the Fourth. He should have been in command all the time. But the truth was, he was lost.

He wanted his own life. Not one that was dictated by rules and the demands of running a country. If he'd made the decision to return to

Alma on his own he might feel differently but right now he felt strong-armed into it.

But somehow in Emily's arms he'd found something.

Emily didn't really feel any better about her next steps, but now that she'd told Rafe her news she could at least start making plans. She didn't know what she expected… Well, the fairy-tale answer was that he'd profess his undying love—hey, their weekend together was pretty spectacular—then sweep her off her feet to his jet, and they'd go to Paris to celebrate their engagement.

But back in the real world, she was staring at him and wondering if this was the last time she'd be alone with him. It didn't matter what the fantasy was or that she knew how he looked naked. They were still strangers.

Intimate strangers.

"You are looking at me in an odd way," he said.

She struggled with her blunt nature. Saying that she knew what he looked like naked but not how he'd react to their child would reveal too much insecurity. So she searched for something light. Keeping things light was the key to this.

"Well, I never heard you rap along with Jay-Z and Kanye before. Sort of changed my opinion of you."

"I'm a man of many talents," he said.

"I'd already guessed that."

"Did you?"

"Yes."

He walked over to her, all sex on a stick with that slow confident stride of his. His hazel eyes were intense, but then everything about him was. Last time they were together, she'd sensed his need to just forget who he was, but this time was different. This time he seemed to want to show her more of the man he was.

The real man.

"What else have you guessed?" he asked in a silky tone that sent shivers down her spine.

He had a great voice. She knew he had flaws, but as far as the physical, she couldn't find any. Even that tiny scar on the back of his hand didn't detract from his appeal. "That you are used to getting your own way."

"Aw, that's so easy it's almost like cheating."

"Have you figured out that I'm used to getting my own way, too?" she asked. Suddenly she didn't feel as if things were just happening to her. She was in control. Of Rafe, the baby and this entire afternoon. The pregnancy had thrown her. Brought up junk from her childhood she'd thought she'd moved on from, but now she was getting her groove back.

"Oh, I knew that from the moment I entered Shady Harry's and saw you standing behind the bar."

"Did you?" she asked. "I thought it was my Shady Harry's T-shirt that caught your attention."

The spicy scent of his aftershave brought an onslaught of memories of him moving over her. She'd buried her face in his neck. Damn, he'd smelled good. Then and now.

"Well, that and your legs. Red, you've got killer legs."

She looked down at them. Seemed kind of average to her. But she wasn't about to argue with a compliment like that.

"I like your ass," she admitted.

He winked at her, and then turned so that she could see it. He wore a slim-fitting suit that looked tailor-made. Given who he was, it probably was.

He was going to be king.

She had no business flirting with him. Or even staying here a moment longer.

"Sorry."

"What?" he asked. "Why? What happened?"

She shrugged. No way was she admitting she was intimidated by his title. But that was the truth. She wasn't in control of that. No matter how much she wanted to be.

"This suit doesn't do anything for me, does it? I asked Gabe if these pants made me look fat but he said no."

She had seen pictures of his entire family in the newspaper and knew that the Gabe he referred to was Gabriel Montoro, his younger brother.

She laughed, as she knew he wanted her to. But inside something had changed. She no longer owned this afternoon. "I should go."

"Why? What happened just now?"

"I remembered that you aren't just a rich guy from Miami who came to Key West for the weekend. That your life isn't your own and I really don't have a place in it."

His expression tightened and he turned away from her. She studied him as he paced over to his bed and looked down at the expensive leather suitcase lying there. She'd interrupted his packing. He probably didn't really have time for her this afternoon.

"You said you never knew your father." With an almost aristocratic expression, he glanced over his shoulder at her. She had the feeling she was seeing the man who would be king. And she had to admit he made her a little bit nervous. Maybe it was simply the fact that she knew he was going to be a king now. But it seemed as if he was different. More regal in his bearing than he had been during their weekend together.

"Yes. I don't see what that has to do with anything."

"I did know my father and my grandfather and great-grandfather. From my birth I was named to follow in their footsteps. I've never deviated from that expectation, and to be honest, I took a certain pride in carrying on our family name and trying to set an example for my brother and sister."

"I'm getting a poor little rich boy feeling here. You have been given a lot of opportunities in your lifetime and now you have the chance to lead a nation," she said, but inside she sort of understood what he was getting at. His entire life had been scripted since birth. She understood from what she'd read in the newspapers that the Montoros may have left Alma in the middle of the night, but they hadn't left their pride behind.

"All my life I've done what is expected of me.

I haven't shirked a single duty. I'm the CEO of Montoro Enterprises and now I will be king of Alma, but for this one afternoon, Red, can I be Rafe? Not a man with his future planned but your lover? Father of your baby?" he asked.

He came back over and dropped to his knees in front of her, wrapping his arms around her hips. Then he drew her closer to him and kissed her belly. "I want you to be able to speak to our baby about me with joy instead of regret."

She looked down at him as he rested his head against her body. Tunneling her fingers into his thick black hair, she understood that from this point on, when she left this penthouse they couldn't be this couple again.

She sighed, and the woman she'd always been, the one who lived by the motto Never Say Never, took over. Rafe and she might not have more than this time together. And she wanted this one last time with him.

She hadn't expected to be a mom this soon. She had made all these plans for her life and then when she'd taken those pregnancy tests it had all gone out the window.

But for this moment she could forget about tomorrow. She hoped this would be enough, but feared one more afternoon in his arms would never be enough to satisfy her.

Two

Rafe pushed aside all of his thoughts and just focused on Emily. It was amazing that she'd come to find him. She was strong enough, independent enough to keep the baby from him if she'd wanted. It embarrassed him a little, humbled him, too, that he would never have known about the baby if she hadn't shown up.

He'd been focusing on the royal legacy and managing everyone's expectations. Especially people he didn't even know and hadn't cared existed until last month. Funny how he'd gone from worrying about financial targets and managing a multinational company to worrying about a little thing like protocol.

But as long as Emily was here he could forget all that. Concentrate on being the man and not the king.

He held her tightly as he stood up, lifting her off her feet and letting her slide back down his body. She was curvy and light, his woman, and he wanted to be just her man. He carried her to the big brass bed and stood next to it, just waiting for a signal from her.

She owed him nothing.

She sighed and then lowered her head and brushed her lips over his, and something tight and frozen inside him started to melt. She kissed him not like the bold bartender she was when they'd met, but like a woman who wanted to relish her time with her lover.

They both knew without saying it that this was the last time they'd be together like this. Maybe if they'd met two years from now after he'd been on the throne and had time to figure out what being king meant, their path would have been different. But they hadn't.

They had this afternoon and nothing more.

He wanted these memories of the two of them to keep for himself as he moved into a life that was no longer his own.

He pushed his hands into her thick red hair, cradling her head as he took control of the kiss. He thrust his tongue deep into her mouth, tasted peppermint and woman. Her arms slipped lower and she stroked her hand down his back as he deepened the kiss.

Though he knew this long, wet kiss was just the beginning, he wanted to savor it. Dueling desires warred inside him as he wanted to make every touch last as long as possible. The intensity of his lust for her was almost unbearable; he needed to be hilt-deep inside her right now.

He lifted his head, rubbed his thumb along the column of her neck. Her pulse was racing and her eyes were half closed. Her creamy skin was dotted with freckles and the faint flush of desire.

He dropped nibbling kisses down her neck. She smelled of orange blossoms and sea breeze. She was like the wildest parts of Florida, and he felt as if he could hold her for only a fleeing moment and then she'd be gone. Tearing through his life like a hurricane.

He slid his hands down her back, tightening them around her waist, and lifted her off her feet again. She wrapped her legs around his waist and put her hands on his shoulders. Then she looked down into his eyes with that bright southern-Atlantic-blue gaze of hers. He felt lost. As if he were drowning in her eyes.

She nipped at his lower lip and then sucked it into her mouth and he hardened. He was going to explode if he didn't get his damned tailored pants off and bury himself in her body.

He reached for his fly but she shifted on him, rubbing her center over his erection. He shook, and the strength left his legs as he stumbled and fell back on the bed. She laughed and then thrust her tongue into his mouth again. And he gave up thinking.

She was like the wildest hurricane and all he could do was ride this storm out. She moved over him and made him remember what it felt like to be alive. The same way she had four weeks ago in Key West. She made the rest of the world pale, and everything narrowed to the two of them.

The heat flared between them and his clothes felt too constricting. He needed to be naked. Wanted her naked. Then she could climb back on his lap. He tore his mouth from hers, his breath heavy as he drew her T-shirt up and over her head and tossed it aside.

She wore the same beige lace bra she'd had on the last time they'd had sex. He traced his finger over the seam where the fabric met skin, saw the goose bumps spread from her breast over her chest and down her arms. Her nipple tightened and he leaned forward to rub his lips over it as he reached behind her back and undid the bra.

The cups loosened, but he didn't lift his head from her nipple. He continued teasing her with light brushes of his tongue over it until she reached between them and undid his tie, leaving it dangling around his neck as she went to work on his shirt buttons.

He shifted back, taking the edge of her bra between his teeth and pulling it away. She laughed, a deep, husky sound he remembered so well. And he got even harder. He had thought there was no way he could want her more, but he'd been wrong.

She pushed the fabric of his shirt open and peeled it down his arms, but she hadn't undone his cuffs so his own shirt bound him. His hands were trapped.

"Undo my hands."

"Not yet, Rafe. Right now, I'm in charge," she said. She scraped her fingernail down the side of his jaw to his neck and then over his pectorals. He sat there craving more of her touch, but damned if he was going to ask her for it. Control and power were two things he always maintained. But with Emily it was as if they'd flown out the window.

She took what she wanted, and though he'd never admit it out loud, he didn't want to stop her. It felt good to just let go.

Flexing her fingers, she dug her nails into his chest and then shifted forward so that the long strands of her hair brushed against him. He shuddered with need, turning his head to try to catch her mouth with his, but she just laughed again and shifted back on his thighs, looking down at him with those eyes that were full of mysteries he knew he'd never really understand.

She drew one finger down the center of his chest, following the path of the light dusting of hair. She swirled her finger around his belly button in tiny circles that made everything inside him contract.

She stroked his erection through the fabric of his pants, and he canted his hips.

She rocked against him and smiled when he moaned her name. Wrapping her arms around his shoulders, she caught the lobe of his ear between her teeth and bit it lightly before whispering all the things she was going to do him. He felt his control slipping with each thrust of her tongue as she flicked it into his ear and then shifted backward on his thighs to reach between them, stroking his length through his pants again.

Cursing, he tried to reach for her but his bound arms wouldn't let him. She rotated her shoulders and rubbed her nipples against his chest. She closed her eyes as she undulated against him, and this time he pulled his arms forward with all of his strength and heard the tear of fabric. She opened her eyes and then started laughing.

He grabbed her waist and rolled to his side, pulling her with him. He rolled over top of her, carefully keeping his weight on his elbows and knees so she wasn't crushed under him. He took both of her hands in his and stretched them high over her head and then rubbed his chest over hers and heard her moan.

Damn, she felt good. Better than he'd remembered her feeling, and that said a lot because he still had erotic dreams of their weekend together.

He lowered his head and sucked her nipple into his mouth, holding both of her wrists above her head with one of his hands. He reached lower between their bodies and undid her jeans, pushing them down so that he could cup her in his hand. He rubbed her mound, and then traced the seam of her panties. Her legs scissored underneath his and he shifted until he lay between them. He let go of her wrists as he slowly kissed his way down her body.

She was covered in freckles; up close he could see that they were all different sizes. He flicked his tongue over each of them as he moved lower and lower until he found her belly button ring. The small loop had a starfish dangling from it. He tongued it and traced the circumference of her belly button.

He moved lower, catching the top of her bikini panties with the tip of his finger and drawing them slowly down. She shifted her hips and he pushed her jeans and panties down to her knees. She kicked them the rest of the way off.

He traced the pattern of freckles from her thigh to her knee, circling her kneecap and the small scar there before caressing his way back up the inside of her thighs. He felt the humid warmth of her body and traced her feminine core with his fingertip. She shifted on the bed, her hands reaching for him, but it was his turn to tease her. Plus if she touched him, he feared his control would splinter into a million pieces and this would be over too quickly.

He parted her folds and then leaned down to taste her. He closed his eyes as he sucked her intimate flesh, causing her to draw her legs closer around him and her hands to fall to the back of his head. She gripped his hair as her hips lifted upward toward his mouth and his tongue.

She was addicting. He couldn't get enough of her. He pushed one finger into her body and heard her call his name. She was wet and ready for him. He fumbled, trying to free himself from his trousers. He lifted his head, looked up at her and saw that she was watching him. Her eyes were filled with passion and desire.

He stood up, shoved his pants and underwear off in a move that definitely couldn't be called graceful, and then he lowered himself on top of her. He slowly used his chest and body to caress hers as he moved over her. She shifted her legs so that her thighs were on either side of his and he moved his hips forward, felt the tip of his erection at the opening of her body. He hesitated. This time was different from their weekend in Key West, but the passion in her eyes was the same.

Slowly he entered her, trying to make it last because she felt so damned good. She gripped his rock-hard flesh as he entered her and drove himself all the way home and then forced himself to stay still once he was fully seated in her body.

Her hands were on his shoulders, running up and down his back and then reaching lower to cup his butt and try to get him to move. But he needed a moment before he did that. A moment to make sure that she was with him. He lowered his head to her neck, and then bit her lightly before moving lower, kissing the full globes of her breasts.

She tightened as she arched underneath him. She looked up at him and whispered dark, sexual words that made his control disappear along with his willpower, and he found himself thrusting deeper into her body. Driving toward his climax and carrying her along with him.

He pushed her legs higher, putting her feet on his shoulders so he could go deeper, and pounded into her faster and faster until he heard her calling out his name and he spilled himself inside her. He thrust into her three more times before he let go of her legs and fell forward, bracing himself on his arms. He kissed the pert pink nipple on her left breast as he rested his head on her shoulder and tried to catch his breath.

He got up and left her for a few moments to wash up and then came back and lay down next to her on the bed. He was aware of the time and knew he should already be at the private airport and getting on his family's jet so he could travel with them to Alma, but he couldn't make himself leave.

He knew that this wasn't love. He wasn't going to lie to her or himself. But she was pregnant with his child and this fired him with an enthusiasm he just couldn't muster when he thought of being king. He didn't want the throne, but his father, who couldn't inherit it because he'd never had his marriage annulled after divorcing Rafe's mother, had been very clear that he thought Rafe needed to do his duty.

He stroked his hand down Emily's arm. She had turned on her side and had her head on his shoulder.

"What are you thinking?"

"That I'm glad you came here today. Did you ever think of not telling me?" he asked.

He suspected he knew the answer, but wanted to hear it from her.

"No. It wasn't easy to track you down—you're pretty secretive about this penthouse bachelor pad, aren't you? But Harry has lots of friends who have connections. It only took him six hours to find you."

"Harry scares me," Rafe admitted. The owner of Shady Harry's bar had been fun and gregarious when Rafe had been partying and buying rounds for the entire place. But the next morning when he'd spotted the older man as he'd left Emily's cottage, Harry had given him a look that said to watch his back. "What's he to you?"

"He and my mom dated for a while," Emily said. "He's sort of like my stepdad. Why?"

"I have a feeling if I show up in Key West he's going to be waiting with a shotgun."

"You're not going to Key West, you're going to Alma. I've seen pictures. It's really beautiful," she said.

Not as beautiful as she was, Rafe thought. He leaned up on his elbow, put his hand flat on her stomach and realized he couldn't control this any more than he could say no to the people in

Alma who'd asked his family to come back and rule the country.

"It is. They've had a rough time since the revolution and I guess...I have to go," he said.

"I know. I told you I wasn't here to ask you to stay. I just needed you to know."

"Why?"

"I didn't know my dad. My mom has never mentioned his name to me. I asked her one time about him and she started crying. I want more than that for our baby. It's not that I had a deprived childhood, but I always wonder. I have this emptiness inside me that nothing can fill. It's that empty spot where everyone else has a dad."

He was humbled by her explanation. He knew he wanted to be more than a name and a face to their kid, though. "We need to figure this out."

There was a knock on the bedroom door.

"Rafael? Are you in here? Your father is in a car waiting downstairs and if you're not down in ten minutes he's coming up here and getting you." It was his personal assistant, Jose.

Jose was his right-hand man at Montoro Enterprises and at home. He took care of all the details.

"I have company," Rafe said. But Emily was more than just company. She was his lover. The mother of his unborn child.

"I am aware of that," Jose said.

"Tell Father I'll be down when I'm down," Rafe said.

But the mood was broken and Emily was getting up and putting her clothes on. She had her jeans on and buttoned, but he stopped her before she put her T-shirt on. He pulled her into his arms. It seemed the sort of gesture that would reassure her, but since he was already thinking of everything he had to do, it felt hollow. He knew she noticed it, too, when she pulled back and shook her head.

The mantle of being a Montoro was tightening around him. "I—"

"Don't. No excuses and definitely no lies,"

she said. She reached into her back pocket and pulled out a business card for Shady Harry's; he turned it over and saw she'd written her name and number on the back. "If you want to know about our child, contact me."

"I do. I will," he said.

She smiled up at him. "I know that the next few weeks are going to be crazy for you, so no pressure."

She pulled her shirt on and then tucked her underwear into her purse and started for the door. He watched her walk out. Part of him wanted to run after her and make her stay so he could talk her into trying a relationship or maybe even marriage. Another part wanted to scoop her up and run away with her to some Pacific island where no one would know their names, far enough away from his family and everyone they knew.

But Emily was a brave sort of woman, and running had never been his style, either, so he had no choice but to get dressed and head down to the car.

His father didn't speak to him the entire way to the airport. Rafael III had wanted the throne enough to try to convince his ex-wife to come back, but Rafe's mother wasn't interested in doing anything to help out her former husband. To say the two of them had a strained relationship was putting it mildly.

They were a prime example of how getting married to the wrong person didn't make for a happy family. Rafe had the childhood to prove it.

During the ride, his cousin Juan Carlos spoke too much. Telling him what was expected of the next king of Alma.

Juan Carlos had been orphaned and seemed to be fixated on the monarchy as a way of proving to himself and the rest of the family that he could carry on his parents' legacy. Perhaps if Rafe's parents hadn't divorced and been horrible to each other, he'd have felt the same way about the family honor.

Rafe freely admitted to himself that if Emily's pregnancy became public knowledge it would create a scandal that would make protecting that legacy even more difficult. But Rafe tuned Juan Carlos out and tried to figure out what he expected of himself as a man.

Three

Key West was a tourist town and there was no getting around that. The atmosphere was laid back and everyone had a sort of hungover look. There was something about being on the edge of the ocean that inspired indulgence in sun, sand and drinks.

Emily sat on the front porch of her flamingo-pink and white cottage with her feet propped on the railing, desperately needing to absorb that laid-back attitude. She'd left Miami and Rafe behind. She'd done what she'd set out to do, namely tell him he was going to be a father. That had gone well—differently than she'd expected, but the end result was the same. She was back here.

Alone.

"Em. Your mom asked me stop by," Harry said as he walked around the side of the house.

He was tall, at least six five, and wore middle age well. His reddish-blond hair had thinned a little but was still thick enough, and he wore it cut short in a military style. His beard was equal parts red, blond and gray, and he had an easy smile. He was the closest thing she had to a dad. So she was glad to see him.

"Why?" Emily asked. Though she knew why her mom had sent Harry. If anyone could make her forget her troubles it was the jovial bar owner.

"She thought you might need some company. She's on her way back to port but won't be here until tonight."

Emily sighed. "I don't really want any company."

"Figured you might say that, so I brought you

a cup of decaf and a blueberry bagel. We can both sit here and eat and pretend we're alone."

Decaf.

Seemed like a little thing, but she always drank full-on caffeine. Now she knew that her mom had spilled the beans about her being preggers. Harry handed her a bakery bag from Key Koffee with the bagel and the coffee.

"You know?"

"I know. It was that slick guy from South Beach, right?"

She tipped her head back and closed her eyes. "He's not that slick."

Harry laughed. "They never are. Talk to me, kiddo. Do I need to take my .45 and head to Miami?"

She opened her eyes and lifted her head. "You would have made a really good dad," she said, smiling at him.

"I think I have been to you," he reminded her.

"You have. But no to the .45. Besides, you'd have to fly to Europe to find him."

Harry took a bite out of his everything bagel

and settled down on the top step, turning sideways with his back against the railing to face her.

"Europe? He seemed American to me," Harry said.

"He's Rafael Montoro IV. Part of…I'm not sure what to call him. But his family was royalty in a tiny Mediterranean country called Alma. They were kicked out decades ago but now they want them back. He's the oldest son and heir apparent to the newly restored monarchy."

"Complicates things, doesn't it?" Harry said.

"You have no idea," she said. "But I didn't expect him to do anything when I gave him the news. You know?"

Harry took a sip of his coffee and then gave her one of those wise looks of his that she hated. He knew when she was lying, especially to herself.

"Okay, fine, I wanted him to be, like, we'll do this together. Instead, I got…he was sweet but clearly torn. He can't let his family down. And he and I only had one weekend together, Harry."

"Sometimes that's all it takes," he said.

"It wasn't enough for the guy who fathered me," she said. "Please don't tell Mom I said that. But really, that complicates everything. I've always thought I was okay with the fact that I don't know who he was, but this baby…" She put her hands on her stomach. "It's making me realize I'm not."

Harry didn't say anything. And after a few minutes Emily looked away from him and back to the foot traffic on the street near her house. What could he say? He was her substitute dad who'd stepped up when he didn't have to. Harry must have thought that she was making a mess where there didn't need to be one.

"I get it, kiddo. It's hard to not want the best for your baby. We all do that," he said. "Try to fix the problems in our past so that our kids don't have to experience them."

"Did you do that for Rita and Danny?" she asked. Harry had two kids who were both more than fifteen years older than her and lived in Chicago. They came down for two weeks each spring to visit Harry.

"I tried. But I ended up making my own mistakes and they have done the same. It's all a part of being human," he said.

"I'm getting Zen Harry this morning," she said. But his positive attitude helped take her mind off Rafe and the sadness she'd been feeling.

It wasn't that she'd expected anything else from him, but that she'd wanted something more. She shook her head as she realized that what she'd wanted was to be wanted.

For him to want to stay with her.

It was unrealistic, but a girl could dream.

"Well, I do have all this wonderful advice and no one to share it with," Harry said with a wink. "You'll be okay, kiddo. You'll make decisions and choices and some of them are going to be fabulous and others you're going to regret. But I do know one thing."

"What's that?" she asked.

"You're going to love that baby of yours, and in the end that's all that really matters."

"You think so?"

"I do. Your own mom did that for you. Look how you turned out," he said.

"Not bad," she admitted. She liked her life. She could have followed her mom into a similar career—she was a marine biologist—but Emily liked being on the land and not out at sea. She had a degree in hotel and restaurant management and one day hoped to open her own place. She knew she had a good life, but a part of her still missed Rafe.

Another part of her knew she just missed the idea of Rafe. So far every time they'd been together they'd ended up in bed. It wasn't as if he was even a friend.

She wanted that picture-perfect family that she kept in her head. She wanted that for this baby she was carrying. She didn't want her child to have the piecemeal family that she did. No matter that she loved her mom and Harry fiercely. For her child she wanted more.

And being the bastard of a European king probably wasn't what her child would want. She was going to have to be very protective. Raise the baby to know its own strength and place in the world.

She noticed Harry watching her, realized she wasn't alone and that made the loneliness she felt when she thought of Rafe a little less painful.

Alma was breathtakingly beautiful. The island was surrounded by sparkling blue seas and old world charm seemed to imbue every building. They'd landed at a private air field and were driving to the royal palace in the urban capital of Del Sol.

Rafe had heard there was a lively nightclub scene and before Emily's visit had sort of thought of checking it out. But now that he had the dual mantle of monarchy and fatherhood hanging over him, he figured he should rethink that.

Del Sol was even more striking than the black

and white photos he'd seen in the albums his *tia* Isabella kept. While there were modern buildings dotted throughout the city many of the old buildings remained. Tia Isabella had been a young woman when she'd been forced to flee Alma with the rest of their family. When Rafe and his siblings and cousin had been growing up they'd been entertained by her stories. Tia Isabella had spent a lot of time talking about the old days and what it had been like to grow up on Alma. But Rafe thought he understood why his grandfather hadn't talked that much about it. Rafe would have been sad to leave this homeland, too.

As the royal motorcade made its way into Del Sol, Alma's capital, people on the streets craned their necks to get a glimpse of the Montoros. Rafe was used to a certain level of fame and notoriety in Miami, but not this. There he was one of the jet-set Montoros. The young generation who worked hard and played harder.

Here he was the future monarch. He'd be the face of Alma to the world. And while his ego was sort of jazzed about that, another part of him wasn't.

"Maybe you should put the window down and do that princess wave," his sister Bella said with a sparkle in her blue eyes. Their father and the rest of their party were in a separate vehicle.

"Princess wave? That's more your cup of tea," he said. "Maybe I'll throw up the peace sign."

She giggled. He'd always been close to his little sister, and making her laugh helped him to relax.

Bella looked like a fairy-tale princess with her pretty blond hair. Not anything like Emily. He wondered what Emily would think of Alma. It was an island not that unlike her hometown of Key West, but the laid-back attitude in the Keys was a world away from this charming European nation.

For a country that had been ruled by a dictator for decades, the people in the streets seemed happy and prosperous and the buildings were clean and well-maintained. Rafe didn't see any signs of financial ruin. But economic danger lurked whenever there was a change of regime. And if there was one thing he was good at, it was making money.

But would the government here listen to him?

To be honest he wasn't the kind of person to negotiate for what he wanted. That was one of the reasons Montoro Enterprises had thrived under his leadership. He made bold decisions. Sometimes they didn't pay off, but most of the time they did.

"You okay?" Bella asked.

He started to shrug it off. There was no way he was going to mention Emily or the fact that she was pregnant to his sister. Not until he had a chance to figure it out for himself. But the family stuff was also getting to him, especially how Juan Carlos was going really crazy about protocol and proper image and all that.

"This return to Alma is throwing me," he admitted to her.

"How?" she asked. "You've always handled whatever the family has dished out. This will be no different. Pretend you're the CEO of the country."

As if. Being the king was a "name only" position. No power. Maybe that was why he hesitated to fully embrace it. He was a man of action. Not a figurehead.

"Good suggestion," he said, glancing out the window as they approached the castle. Surrounded by glittering blue water on three sides, it rose from the land like a sand castle at the beach. He groaned.

"What?"

"I was hoping the castle would be in disrepair."

"Why?"

"So I could hate it."

Bella laughed again. "I love it. It's everything I thought it would be," she said.

"What if there's not a hopping club scene? Will you still love it then?" he asked. Bella liked to party. Hell, they all did. They hadn't been raised to assume the throne. They were all more likely to show up in the tabloids in a compromising position than on the society pages at a formal tea. The closer he got to the throne the less sure he was that he wanted to be there.

He felt Bella's hand on his shoulder. "You're going to be fine. I think you'll make a great king."

"Why? I'm not sure at all."

"You've been a great big brother and always ensured our family's place in business and in society."

"Business is easy. I understand that world," Rafe countered.

"I never thought the day would come when you'd admit that you aren't sure of yourself," she said, taking her phone from her handbag.

"What are you doing?"

"Texting Gabe that you have feet of clay."

"He already knows that."

"We all do," Bella said. "Why are you acting like you are just figuring it out?"

"I'm going to be a king, Bella. It's making me nutty," he said.

"You weren't as thrown by it a week ago," she

said. "What happened yesterday to make you delay your flight?"

Nothing.

Everything.

Something that could change the man he was. If he let it.

"Business. Running Montoro Enterprises does take a lot of time," he said.

The car pulled to a stop and an attendant in full livery came to open the door for them. Bella climbed out first but looked back at Rafe.

"Lying to me is one thing. You can keep your secrets if you want to," she said. "But I hope you aren't lying to yourself."

He followed her out of the car, and the warm Mediterranean air swept around him. She had a point. He knew in his gut that this didn't feel right. He should be in Miami with Emily. He missed her.

The porte-cochere led to an inner brick-lined courtyard. There was a fountain underneath a statue of Rafe's great-grandfather Rafael I. He was surprised it hadn't been torn down when the dictator had taken over. Bella stopped walking and spun around on her heel, taking in the beauty of the palace.

For the first time he felt a sense of his royal lineage settling over him. If their family hadn't been forced to flee he would have grown up in this palace. His memories would be of this place that smelled wonderfully of jasmine and lavender. Where was the scent coming from?

His father came up beside him and put his hand on his shoulder not saying a word. Something passed between them. An emotion that Rafe didn't want to define. But Alma became real to him. In a way that it hadn't been before. In Miami it had been easy to say he wasn't sure if he wanted to be king but seeing this palace— he felt the history. And he sort of understood Juan Carlos's perspective for once. Rafe didn't want to let down their family line.

If Alma wanted the Montoros back on the throne than Rafe would have to put aside the feelings he felt stirring for Emily and figure out how to be their king.

That surprised him. He hadn't expected to feel this torn. He was isolated from the rest of his family who seemed to think this return to royalty was just the thing they needed. They were all caught up in being back in the homeland. But as much as he felt swept up in the majesty of their return to Alma he knew he was still trying to figure out where home really was.

Emily worked the closing shift at Harry's and walked home at 2:00 a.m. Key West wasn't like the mean streets of Miami, but she moved quickly and kept her eyes open for danger. It was something she'd teach her kid.

She was starting to find her bearings with this pregnancy more and more as each day passed. Being a mom was going to take some getting used to, but as her own mom had said, she had nine months to make the adjustment.

Her cell phone vibrated in the pocket of her jeans and she reached back to pull it out. Glancing at the screen, she saw it was an international call. She only knew one person who was traveling internationally right now. She did some quick math and figured out that it was early morning in Alma.

"Hello?"

"Hey, Red. Figured you'd be getting off work. Please tell me I didn't wake you." Sure enough, it was Rafe.

"You'd think you'd be more careful about disturbing a pregnant woman's rest," she teased. She didn't want to admit it but she'd missed him. Three days. That was all it had been since she'd seen him, but it had felt like a lifetime. His voice was deep and resonated in her ear, making her feel warm all over.

"Well, maybe I did call the bar earlier to determine if you were working tonight," he admitted.

That sounded like Rafe. He was a man who left little to chance. "What can I do for you?"

"How are you feeling?" he asked. "How's Florida?"

"I'm feeling fine," she said. "I have had a little bit of morning sickness, and it's not just limited to mornings. I've been getting sick mid-afternoon."

She saw her house at the end of the lane and got her keys out. She'd left the porch lights on and it looked so welcoming. The only thing that would be better was if Rafe was waiting for her. And to be honest, as he talked to her on the phone, it was almost as if he was there with her.

"Makes sense since that's when you wake up," he said. "Is there anything you can do to help that?"

"No," she said. "It's not too bad. How's Alma?"

"Nice. You'd like it. It's all sand and sea for as far as the eye can see and quaint little villages. Not as laid back as Key West but still nice."

"Any places to go paddleboarding?"

"Not yet. Why, do you think you'd move here and start a business?" he asked.

It was the closest he'd come to suggesting that she be near him in the future, and she felt numb even contemplating it. She had her own plans to open a restaurant around the corner from

Harry's. Not to be Rafe's hidden mistress in some far-off European country.

"Not at all. I've got a place picked out for my future restaurant," she said.

"Is that what you want to do?"

Once again she realized how little they actually knew of each other's lives.

"Well, I can't be a bartender forever."

"I guess not. Tell me about your dreams," he said.

She thought she heard the sound of footsteps on a tiled floor on his end. "Where are you?"

"Not ready to share that much with me?" he asked, countering her evasion.

In a way she wished they were playing a game. It would make everything easier. She could concentrate on winning and not really have to think about the emotions. But the truth was she was tired and still a little unsure of what she was doing. Sure, just hearing Rafe's voice made her feel not so alone. But she didn't want to allow herself to become dependent on him.

Not to turn her life into one big sob story, but

usually when she started to feel comfortable with someone they left. It wasn't that they abandoned her, just moved on and left her to her independent self. Even her mom and Harry. And she didn't want that with Rafe.

"Nope. I want to hear about Alma. I read a little online yesterday. Seems like the change of regime is going to have a big impact on the economy. I know you are good at making money. Is that why they chose you and your family to come back and lead the country?" she asked.

"Our family ruled the country before the coup that installed the late dictator, Tantaberra. That's why we were chosen. But my parents are divorced so Dad, who would be next in line, can't assume the throne. They want someone with the right pedigree and the right reputation."

"Um…I'm guessing if they found out about me that could put a wrench in things."

"Possibly. I'm not going to deny you exist, Emily."

"Really?"

"Yes. Would I be on the phone with you if I didn't care?" he asked.

"I don't know," she said honestly. "We're strangers."

"Who are about to be parents to a baby," he said. "Let's get to know each other. And while we have half the world between us maybe I can talk to you without being distracted by your body and that sexy way you tilt your head to the side. You always make me forget everything except wanting to get you naked."

Her breath caught as she sank down into the big armchair where Rafe had sat the one time he'd been to her place. They'd made love in the chair and she felt closer to him now. She tucked her leg up underneath her and let those memories wash over her.

"Red? You still there?"

"Yes. Dammit, now you've got me thinking about you naked."

"Good. My evil plan worked," he said. "Tell me something about yourself."

"What?"

"Anything. I want to know the woman who's going to be the mother of my child."

She thought about her life. It was ordinary: nothing too tragic, nothing too exciting. But it was hers. "When I was six I thought if I spent enough time in the ocean I'd turn into a mermaid. My mom's a marine biologist and we were living on her research vessel, *The Sea Spirit*. She made me a bikini top out of shells and sent me off every day to swim."

"I'm glad you didn't turn into a mermaid," he said with a quiet laugh.

They talked on the phone until Emily started drifting to sleep. She knew she should hang up, but she didn't want to break the connection. Didn't want to wake up without Rafe.

"Red?"

"Yes?"

"I wish I was there to tuck you into bed," he said.

"Me, too," she admitted. Then she opened her eyes as she realized that she was starting to need him.

"Good night, Rafe," she said, hanging up the phone before she could do anything stupid like ask him what he'd wanted to be as a boy. Or to come back to Key West.

Four

Rafe secluded himself from the rest of the family in the office area of the suite of rooms he'd been given. The deal he'd struck for Montoro Enterprises to ship Alma's oil was taking a lot of his time.

Alma was a major oil producing country to the north of Spain. Montoro Enterprises would be shipping the oil to its customers in North and South America where the bulk of their business interests were. It made good business sense but he also wanted it because he'd get a chance to explore the country of his ancestors. When he'd first done the deal he'd anticipated his father becoming King not himself.

Plus truth be told, he'd been so focused on work because he was avoiding his family and the coterie of diplomats who seemed to be lurking whenever he stepped out of his suite. He didn't want to talk about his coronation or about the business of running the government. Yet.

But sitting around and hiding out went against the grain, so he'd been working nonstop. He hadn't shaved in the three days, and Mozart had replaced Jay-Z and Kanye on the stereo because no one would ever be tempted to stop working and rap to Mozart. He hadn't even contacted Emily, though he'd thought of her night and day.

She was an obsession. He knew that. He had the feeling that if he were in Miami maybe it wouldn't be as fierce, but he was far away from her and thinking of her was nice and comforting in the midst of this storm that was brewing around him.

He banged his head on the desk.

"I can see I'm interrupting," Gabe said as he entered without knocking.

"I'm working."

"Yeah, I noticed," Gabe said, nodding toward the empty cans of Red Bull that littered the desk and the floor. He walked to the window and pulled back the drapes.

Rafe blinked against the glare of the sunlight. "What time is it?"

"Four in the afternoon. You're expected for dinner tonight and if you don't show up Juan Carlos is going to have a stroke. I know he's been a pain lately with all this royal protocol, but we don't want our cousin to have a stroke, do we?"

Rafe shook his head. "No." He scrubbed his hands over his face. His eyes felt gritty and the stubble on his jaw felt rough. He was a mess. Truly. "This sucks."

Gabe laughed that wicked, low laugh that Rafe had heard women found irresistible. He just found it annoying.

"Yeah, it does. Not so cool being the older brother now, is it?"

Not at all. "I should walk away…that would leave you holding the bag."

A fleeting glimpse of panic ran across his brother's face. "Dad would disown you. I'm pretty sure the board would fire you from Montoro Enterprises. Then what would you do?"

Run away to Key West.

Seemed simple enough, but to be fair he wasn't sure what type of reception he'd receive if he just showed up on Emily's doorstep.

"I think I'm too American to want to be a royal, you know? Maybe Dad still wants it, but it feels weird to me. I don't want to be called 'Your Majesty' or 'Your Highness.'"

Rafe watched his younger brother. If there were the slightest sign that Gabe was interested in being king, Rafe would just walk away and let his brother have it. But Gabe rubbed the back of his neck as he paced over to the window. "Me neither."

"Then I guess I'd better stop acting like a jerk and get out there," Rafe said. "What's the plan?"

"Dinner with some supporters. And a family who'd love for you to meet their daughter," Gabe said with a wry smile.

Rafe shook his head. He'd do his duty to his family, but he was already involved with a redhead who wouldn't take kindly to him catting around. He was getting to know her, starting a relationship with the woman who was going to be the mother of his child. What if she didn't feel possessive toward him the way he did toward her? And he did feel possessive. Emily was his. "I'm not interested."

"Are you interested in someone else?"

"It's complicated, Gabe."

"I never thought I'd see the day when you said that. Is she special?"

"She could be," Rafe said. Or at least that was what his gut was saying. The rest of him wasn't too sure.

Once his brother left and Rafe had wrapped up what he was working on for the day, he started getting ready for the state dinner. When he got out of the shower, he saw that he had a text message from Emily.

It's official. Just got word back from the doctor's office. I'm due in January.

Would he be able to get back to the States in January?

Being with Emily would mean giving up the monarchy... and possibly his job, depending on how much it pissed off his family. Montoro Enterprises and Alma were now all linked together. Could he walk away from one without walking away from them all?

But what kind of man walked away from his own child?

Not one that Rafe wanted to be. He knew that but as he'd said to Gabe earlier, it was complicated.

He braced his hands on the bathroom counter and looked into his own hazel eyes searching for answers or a solution. But there was nothing there.

And that really pissed him off. He needed to take control of his personal life the way he did the boardroom. No more doing what everyone else wanted unless it fit with his own inner moral compass.

Except that he'd been a playboy for so long he wasn't too sure he had one. Everyone had one, right? Then shouldn't the answer be clearer than this?

When he was finished shaving, he took the towel off his hips and tossed it at his image in the mirror before he walked into the bedroom to dress.

He hit the remote for his sound system and switched from Mozart to "The Man" by Aloe Blacc . He stopped in his tracks. Right now it seemed as if everyone had a piece of him and the man Rafe had always wanted to be had been lost.

He knew what he had to do. No use pretending he was going to do anything else. It wasn't that he thought the path would be easy, but then when had he ever taken the easy path? It was simply that spending time with his siblings made him realize that family was important to him.

His mind made up, he grabbed his phone and began typing, hitting Send before he could have second thoughts.

I'll be there. When is your next appointment? I'd like to go with you if I can.

He owed it to himself and to his child to at least see if he could be a real partner to Emily. And be a real part of the baby's life.

Really? Okay. If you do this then I don't want you making promises you can't keep.

That right there showed him how little she knew of him. Hell, what did he know about her? He knew how she looked in his arms. He knew that she had wanted to be a mermaid when she was little. He smiled at that one. He knew she was having his baby.

I'm a man of my word, Red. I'll be there.

* * *

Two days later Emily woke up to a beautiful sunny morning. Since it was her day off, she decided to take her paddleboard and head to a quiet cove on Geiger Key where there weren't many tourists. She'd been too much in her head since she'd found out she was pregnant and needed to forget for a few hours.

After she'd had her daily bout of morning sickness, she took the prenatal vitamins the doctor had prescribed and then got dressed in her usual bikini. She stood in front of the full-length mirror mounted on the back of her walk-in closet door and looked at her body. No signs of her pregnancy were visible. In fact, she looked a little bit thinner than she had before. Her boobs were getting a little larger, though.

She'd always sort of been…well, smallish, but now she was actually filling out the top. Not bad, she thought. She patted her stomach and shook her head. She definitely needed today for herself.

Someone knocked on her front door. She

grabbed her board shorts, putting them as she went to answer it.

There was a man in a suit waiting there.

"Hello, Ms. Fielding. I have a package for you from Rafael Montoro. He asked me to deliver it to you personally."

She took the package from him. "You look a little fancy for a deliveryman."

"I'm Jose, his assistant at Montoro Enterprises," Jose said.

"That explains the suit," she said.

She wanted to ask more questions, debated it for a moment, and then decided to heck with looking cool. "So when will he be back in the US?"

"I'm not at liberty to say."

"Really? He sent you here but you can't tell me that?" she asked. "I know it's your job to protect his privacy, it's just that he said…never mind. Thank you for getting up early to deliver this. Are you driving back to Miami?"

"Nah. I took the company chopper."

Of course he did. Men like Rafe—and his

assistant, for that matter—didn't drive almost four hours to Key West like other mere mortals.

"Safe travels," she said, turning around to go back inside.

What had he sent her?

"Ms. Fielding?"

She glanced over her shoulder at Jose. "He's hoping to be back next week but that all depends on the people in Alma."

She smiled at him. "Thank you."

"Don't rat me out," he said with a wink, and then left.

His assistant was nice. She wondered if that was a reflection of Rafe as a boss, but she knew no matter who worked for him he might still be a jerk at work. "Jose!"

"Yes."

"What kind of man is Rafe to work for?"

"Demanding. He won't settle for a job half done. But he's also very generous when a project is over. He's a good man," he said.

"Thanks," she said.

He walked away and she thought about it. A

good man. Was she a good woman? Hell, yes, she was. She sat down on what she was now calling the Rafe chair and opened the package. When she pulled back the sides of the cardboard box there was a pretty paper inside with the words *Handcrafted in Alma* printed on it in scrolling letters.

She carefully pulled the sides of the paper back to reveal something in Bubble Wrap. Lifting it from the box, she carefully removed the Bubble Wrap and caught her breath as she saw that it contained a stained glass mermaid that looked a lot like her.

She traced her finger over the details and tried to downplay the importance of the gift. But she couldn't avoid the fact that he'd taken her childhood dream and given it to her.

She took a picture and then attached it to the text message.

She's even prettier than I imagined a mermaid could be. Thank you for this wonderful gift.

The response was almost instantaneous.

I'm glad you like it. I'm just coming out of a meeting. Do you have time to chat with me?

She thought about the paddleboarding she'd planned for the day, but as her mom always said, the ocean wasn't going anywhere. Plus a part of her realized she'd been running away from her house and her situation so she didn't have to deal with it on her own. Talking to Rafe was a solution. She didn't want it to be, because she'd always prided herself on being independent and handling anything life threw at her. But she knew she wanted him by her side.

Yes. I can talk.

Good. I'll call in a few minutes.

She paced around her living room and ended up back in the kitchen. She took the stained glass mermaid and held her up to the back window, where she got the light from the morning sun, and realized she'd fit perfectly there.

She jotted down the supplies she'd need and then made herself a mango and passion fruit smoothie. By the time she was finished with it, he still hadn't called.

He was a man who would be king, she thought. Obviously his time wasn't his own. She waited another thirty minutes before she turned the ringer off on her phone, got into her car and drove to Geiger Key.

She tried to shake it off. She'd known that the only one she could count on was herself, but it stung just the tiniest bit that he hadn't messaged her back to say he'd been delayed.

Rafe was in a bad mood by the time he escaped the royal palace in Del Sol and drove down the winding coastal road to his family's beach compound in Playa del Onda. He'd spent the entire day either in meetings or being cornered by Dita Gomez.

Dita was the oldest daughter of one of the best families in Alma. Her parents were part of the newly forming royal court and they were hoping for a royal match. Dita was a lovely lady, no doubt, but as his man Kanye might say, she was a gold digger. Rafe wasn't entirely sure how she had access to his schedule but everywhere he went, she was there.

He'd been so busy dealing with getting rid of Dita that he hadn't been able to call Emily. And he knew her well enough to know that giving the excuse that he'd been dodging the advances of a beautiful blonde wasn't going to go over well.

Wanting to punch something, he shoved his hands in his hair. This was too restricting. He hadn't felt a connection to Alma or to the people the way that Bella seemed to. While he was busy plotting ways to get back to Miami early, she was happy to stay for a little while longer.

He wondered if something had happened to make Bella so happy with the land that time forgot. He made a mental note to talk to her, but he had no idea when he'd get a chance. His schedule was grueling.

He glanced at his watch; it had been seven hours since he said he'd call Emily. That meant it was probably midafternoon in Key West. He dialed her number and waited. It rang twice before he got a text message that had obviously been tailored for him saying she didn't want to talk to His Majesty.

First he was angry. Screw her. He was doing his best to keep all the balls in the air. Family, business, kingdom. He'd expect her to understand.

Then he remembered what she'd said to him a few days ago. *Don't make promises he couldn't keep.*

So he dialed her number again and this time she answered. But she didn't say anything— all he heard was the rush of wind and the faint sound of music in the background.

"Don't hang up. I'm sorry. My days over here are insane and I ended up being cornered by someone from the royal court. This is the first time I've been alone since I texted you."

After an excruciating pause, she finally spoke. "It's okay. I know you're busy. But even busy men can take a moment to text."

"Point taken. Honestly, Em, I feel like I'm

running from one thing to the next and I can't catch up. I'm not used to this. And I feel like I have to play nice and by their rules. This means a lot to my family."

That was the problem. He wanted to tell them what he'd do and then say take it or leave it. But that wasn't an option. Tia Isabella was so excited to be returning home. He couldn't and wouldn't disappoint his great-aunt or any of his other relatives by ruining this for them. They'd looked to him for leadership and he was stepping up.

But he was losing himself.

"I'm trying to figure this out."

"Who says you have to do it all?" she asked. "Being the monarch and the head of a huge company is a big task for anyone. I think in most countries that isn't allowed."

"I know. But I like running the company. There I'm only answerable to the board and I have a certain degree of anonymity to deal with problems on my own. Here...I sat in a meeting today about what color napkins we should have at the coronation."

She laughed. "What color did you decide?"

"I have no idea. I tuned out," he said. "I'd never do that at a board meeting."

"Well," she said at last. "I'm no expert on that sort of thing but I think you're going to have to find what makes being king exciting to you. I bet at Montoro Enterprises there are tasks that would normally bore you but you do them because you want to be successful."

She was right. "Good advice."

"Thanks. And thank you again for the mermaid. I hung her up after I got back from paddleboarding and am looking forward to seeing my kitchen lit up when the sun sets tonight."

"I wish I was there with you," he said.

"Don't."

"Don't what?"

Don't say things like that. Let's keep this light," she said. "That way I don't start thinking something else and you don't have to worry about calling me."

Hell. "I do want to call you, Em. I like talking to you and you make me…you're the only thing that feels real right now."

"That's because I have nothing to do with Alma or the throne. And you know with me it's just about the baby and getting to know each other. But that's running away from your obligations in Alma. And I think that for a little while that might suit you, but eventually it won't."

"I'm not sure what you mean by that," he said. Afraid very much that he did know what she meant.

"That once you decide to commit to Alma and the people there, you will realize that you can't have me. I'll have been the distraction you needed to make the decision, and then I'll be left by the wayside."

Damn. He knew she was right. He didn't want to admit it to her, but then with Emily he didn't have to. "That's not my intention."

"Whether that's true or not, you can't change who you are and with you, Rafael Montoro IV, it's all about your family legacy. And we both know you aren't going to turn your back on it."

She was right. She'd taken the debate he'd been having with himself and boiled it down to its essence. He was a man who was all about family; it was the compass he used in every decision he'd ever made. Now he just had to decide if he could shift away from the Montoro legacy to pursue his own future with Emily and their child. And the decision would be a tough one.

After he hung up with her he went to his office to work. He put on a little Jimmy Buffett because he needed to hear some sounds of home.

There was a knock on the door and he rubbed the back of his neck. "Come in."

"Sir, I have a few more questions for the coronation," Hector said as he entered. Hector was the head of the Coronation Committee. Since Alma hadn't had a monarch in several decades, they were anxious to make sure the coronation had all the bells and whistles.

"Please have a seat," Rafe said. This was what he'd be giving up, he thought as Hector talked about where foreign dignitaries would be seated. Alma was going to be a world player. Lots of countries were interested in doing business with them since their previous ruler had kept the country isolated. Rafe's skills in business made him uniquely suited to help Alma get the most from their entry into the global marketplace.

"Do you like that?"

Rafe had to start paying attention. As Emily said, he needed to find the things about it that excited him. "You know better than me, Hector. No offense, but I'm not at all interested in color schemes or seating arrangements."

"None taken. You're a man of action and need to be doing something," Hector said.

"True. I'm going to let you make all the choices. If something doesn't look right then I will tell you."

"Thank you, sir."

"Clearly you know what you're doing," Rafe said.

Hector stood up to leave, but turned back when he got to the door. "I mean, thank you for coming back here. It means a lot to our people."

Hector left.

Rafe felt humbled. He knew that he wasn't going to find it easy to choose between Alma and Emily. He needed her and the people needed him.

Five

"I toured the countryside today. I have to say that it is beautiful. There's a little cove that I know you would like," Rafe said.

It was 10:00 a.m. Emily sat at one of the corner tables in the coffeehouse on Duval Street talking to Rafe. It had become their date. He hadn't missed calling her one time since the day he'd sent the stained glass mermaid a week ago. She hated to admit it, but she looked forward to his calls every day.

She took a sip of her herbal tea and looked out the window, but she didn't see Key West. Instead she saw the countryside of Alma as he described the rolling hills and hedgerows. The sheep on the hillside munching on grass.

"How's the weather there?" she asked. "I've never been farther north than Georgia."

"It's nice. The island isn't that big and so the sea breezes keep it cool. I think you'd like it."

He said that almost every time they talked, but she'd read the papers and online articles and knew there was no way she could ever visit him there. There was even speculation online that he'd chosen a bride from one of Alma's aristocratic families. She knew that came with the territory of being a monarch.

"Met any nice locals?" she asked before she could stop herself.

"A few. The head of the Coronation Committee is a great guy. He's helped me find things I like to do," he said.

She noticed he didn't mention any women, even though she'd seen his picture with more than one. It still made her sad.

Not sad enough that she stopped taking his calls or looking forward to talking to him.

She suddenly understood how a woman could willingly become a man's mistress. Because she had the feeling that if he asked her to, she'd be tempted to say yes. She was falling for him and he wasn't even here with her. But the silly thing was it was more intense by not actually having him physically here. They didn't argue over the little things like what to get for dinner because they only had a few hours together each week, and then it was only by phone.

"You still there?"

"Yes," she said. "Just imagining Alma."

"What's your view like today?"

"Sunburned tourists in swimsuits and flip-flops. There was a guy last night at the bar who had a few too many and kept coming on to this group of coeds. They ignored him and so he started stripping. Can you imagine? I was laughing because he was harmless. A sunburned middle-aged man. I wanted to see how far he'd go. But Harry put an end to it."

"Sounds interesting. Did you think he'd look good naked?" Rafe asked.

"Nah. He didn't look anything like you. It was the expression on his face that had me hooked. He wasn't going to stop until those women acknowledged him."

"So he didn't look like me... Does that mean you like the way I look naked?" Rafe asked. "Because I haven't slept a single night without remembering how you felt in my arms that last time in Miami."

She took a sip of her tea and put her feet up on the chair across from her. She'd thought of little else but the way Rafe looked with his shirt off or how he'd moved when he'd been rapping to Jay-Z in his bedroom at the penthouse. She hadn't realized that she could be so lusty with this pregnancy, but she was.

"Tell me about it," she said.

"I will tonight. Why don't you call me when you get off work? I'll be waiting up for you."

She liked the sound of that. She glanced around the coffeehouse and noticed a man watching her. He looked away as she spotted him. Weird.

"Okay. I'm working an early shift because Harry is worried that late nights aren't good for me."

"They probably aren't. As a matter of fact, why don't you quit your job there?"

"Why would I do that?" she asked. She'd be bored stiff if she had nothing to do, and her savings would only last her three months. Then she'd have to look for another job. Though she knew Harry would take her back.

"I don't like the idea of you working late nights," he said. "I can support you so you don't have to work."

She put both feet on the floor and leaned forward as a wave of annoyance swept over her. "I don't need your money, Rafael. I'm not about to become your kept woman."

"Slow down, Red. I just meant that if you are tired, I'd help you out. It's nothing any man wouldn't do for the woman carrying his baby."

"That's not true," she said. Her own father had done a lot less. He'd just walked away and left her mom and her alone. "I guess you hit one of my triggers. I don't do needy."

"Hell, I know that. I don't do overprotective usually, but with you I want to. I know that's not what you want from me, so I'm keeping my distance," he said.

"Yeah, right, you're 'keeping your distance' because of your obligation to your family. You're just as afraid of committing yourself to me as you are of committing yourself to the throne."

There was silence on the line and she wondered if she'd gone too far. A part of her almost wished she had because then he'd just break it off with her and she'd know she was on her own.

These calls, this bond that was developing between them couldn't last. She knew it and if Rafe was being honest he'd admit to it too. The way things stood, they couldn't co-parent their child. Didn't royal babies have nannies or something?

She was going to be a hands-on mom and

every time she talked to Rafe she fell a little more for him, started to picture him as a hands-on dad.

"You're right," he said. "But I'm also not rushing back to your side because if I do I'm not sure what sort of reception I'll get."

"What sort do you want?" she asked. She had no idea how she'd act if he showed up on her doorstep, but frankly she imagined she'd be tempted to throw herself into his arms. And she had no idea how he'd react to that.

"You."

She caught her breath. "You don't have to keep this much distance between us, you know."

"I know. But you are unpredictable and I'm not on solid ground right now. Just know I wouldn't be calling you this often if you weren't important to me."

He didn't have to keep quite as much distance as he was for her sake. But getting to know him this way was safer. That was one of the issues she kept pushing to the back of her mind. "Okay, sorry for overreacting. It's just…a lot of things are changing in my body. You know how scary that is for a control freak like me?"

"I do. Red, that's how I feel about this entire constitutional monarchy thing in Alma."

She laughed. He was the only man she knew who'd compare being king to being pregnant. Mainly because he was the only man she knew who wasn't afraid to admit that he had doubts. That he liked to control things. That he was human. He didn't front with her and she knew that was one of the reasons she liked him.

"Okay, so about this late-night call. What do you say we use that video chat function? I miss seeing you," she admitted.

"Finally. I thought you'd never admit to missing me."

"I guess you're not as smart as everyone gives you credit for being," she said.

"Probably not," he said. "But I'm not concerned with what anyone thinks about me but you."

Those words made her heart beat a little faster and made her feel all warm and fuzzy inside.

It wasn't love. Not yet. But she knew if he kept calling her every day she was going to start really falling for him, and she was starting to struggle to remember why that was a bad idea.

After hanging up with Emily, Rafe left the royal palace in Del Sol and walked around the well-manicured gardens. As he walked, he had his iPod set to his Key West playlist, which was really his Emily playlist. But he knew better than to actually name it that—he didn't want to leave any evidence of his affair for others to observe.

He listened to Jack Johnson sing about waking up and making banana pancakes together. Pretending the world outside didn't exist. And Rafe wanted that. But then as the days went by and he met more people in Alma he started to see how much the country needed him, or at least his family, here, too. Rafe guessed they were all so relieved to have the monarchy back.

After years under a dictator he understood that. It was sort of how he'd felt when he'd turned eighteen and left his father's house. He had acted like a wild man in college for about three months before he realized that he wanted his life to be about more than tabloid headlines. So he'd gotten serious and proven to himself that he could stand outside of his father's shadow and still be a part of the family.

"Hey, big brother," Bella said, coming up behind him and linking her arm through his. He pulled his earbuds out and smiled down at his baby sister. She'd really thrived in Alma and had an affinity with the people here that bordered on mutual admiration. For the Montoros, and Juan Carlos in particular, it was as if they'd come home. They were a part of Alma and Juan Carlos was busy bringing them back into the fold. There was sincere joy in all of them at being here. Even Rafe. Though he was torn, with his love of Miami and his lover in Key West.

"Hello, Bella. What's up?"

She led him to one of the wrought iron benches nestled next to a flowering jasmine bush and sat down. He sat down next to her and looked at his sister for the first time in days. She smiled easily.

"You seem distracted lately and I'm going to do the meddling kid sister thing and ask why."

"I'm trying to figure out how to be royal after years of being so ordinary," he said. It was his pat answer, and he'd been saying it to himself for so long that when he finally heard it out loud he realized how hollow the words were.

Maybe Bella wouldn't notice.

"Yeah, right," she said. "I'd think you'd have a better excuse than that."

He wasn't in the mood to discuss this with her and started to get up. But she stopped him with her hand on his sleeve.

"I think you have someone back home," she said. "A woman who isn't from here and can't fit into this world."

"I have a lot of women back home," he said.

"Lying to me is one thing," she said with that honesty that made him feel exposed. "But lying to yourself is something else. If you have a woman, then marry her. Then take the throne."

If it were as simple as that he'd do it. But he knew from the meetings he'd been in that a smooth transition was needed. He was expected to marry someone who'd strengthen the Montoros' claim to the throne. Someone who'd make the people of Alma and its enemies believe that the restored monarchy would be around for a long time. That they were the only ones who could return Alma to its former glory.

And a bartender from Key West who didn't know who her father was wasn't going to be approved by the committee.

"Thanks, Bella, but it's not that simple," he said.

"It is if you know what you want."

He realized anew that he was lost. Hearing his little sister boil down his problems and come up with a solution was humbling. But he couldn't do what she suggested. He hadn't even seen Emily since he'd learned he was going to be a father. Their daily calls were great, but he needed to hold her in his arms again. Look into her eyes and see what, if anything, she felt for him.

Aside from lust. Sex between them had been raw and electric since the moment they'd met, and now he had to figure out if what he felt for her was more than that. Was he just using her as an escape to get away from the mantle of kingship that he didn't want? And he *really* didn't want it.

Because if he did it would be easier to make a decision about Em. Force her to take some money from him and set her and the baby up and then keep his distance. But he wanted more than that.

"I...thank you," he said.

"For what? I didn't say anything that you don't already know for yourself. Tell me what's going on."

He shook his head. "You've done enough."

"I have?"

"Yes. I just needed to hear someone else say it. I've been afraid of screwing up and embarrassing the family so I've stopped being myself. I've been trying to be regal and we both know I'm not."

She laughed and punched his shoulder. "You're not succeeding at being regal. I saw you roll your eyes when the Gomezes mentioned what beautiful babies you and Dita would have."

"I thought I showed a lot of restraint by not mentioning that the babies would probably be born with a tail and cloven hooves."

Bella laughed. "You're not that evil."

"Imp, you think it's funny having someone come after you because of your position? Wait until the princess royal or whatever title they decide on for you has to make a good marriage."

"Don't even joke about that, Rafe. I'm too young and pretty to be tied down to a man." She batted her eyelashes.

He hugged her close. "Damned straight. Besides, only one of us should be shackled by this monarchy thing. I'll do what's needed to protect you, Gabe and the rest of our family."

"Don't sacrifice yourself for us. We're stronger than you think we are."

"I know that. But I want you both to be happy."

Emily's shift was long. Her feet hurt and she felt as if she was going to be sick until she stepped outside into the balmy June air. It was only eleven—so not that late—as she walked through the crowds toward her cottage.

She had been looking forward to chatting with Rafe all evening. But once again she'd seen him on the local news on one of the televisions at the bar. He was with a blonde woman and she hoped like hell that it was just for publicity purposes. But a part of her realized that she had no hold on the king of Alma.

But that Rafe was different from the man who she spoke on the phone with and she hadn't asked about the woman because she really didn't want to hear that his obligation to his family might force him to marry someone else.

The US press, especially the local Miami reporters, loved anything to do with royalty and since the Montoros were raised in America, the media were obsessed with them. It seemed she didn't have to try too hard to find out about Rafael, Gabriel and Bella. She learned about the private schools they'd gone to and had seen Rafe's college roommate on CNN talking about how the Montoros were all about family.

She got it. As far as the media were concerned Rafe was going to make a great king. It had been a long time since an American had claimed a foreign throne, and despite the fact that most patriots were all about democracy they did like a fairy-tale story like this now and then.

She rubbed the back of her neck as she let herself into her house. She kicked off her Vans and left the lights off as she walked to her bedroom. She'd wanted him all day. Looked forward to the time when she could be alone and talk to him, and now she wasn't sure.

She wasn't sure how much more of Rafe she could take before he became so embedded in her soul that she wouldn't be able to survive without him.

She was sure part of it was the hormones from being pregnant with his baby. The other part was that she'd never had this kind of interaction with a guy. They talked every day. Most of her boyfriends had been busy with their own lives and had called only when they were horny or lonely.

Which had suited her.

She'd never wanted anything solid and lasting until now.

Until Rafe. And he wasn't available for her to claim.

Her phone rang. She glanced down at the Skype icon and knew that it was Rafe doing what she'd asked: calling her for a video chat this time.

She missed him. She didn't want to.

But she swiped her finger across the screen, unlocking the phone to answer the call. The image on the other end was dark with just a pool of light in the background.

Her own image popped up as a dark square

in the bottom corner of the screen. She hadn't turned on the light.

"I guess you changed your mind about seeing me," he said.

"I just got home," she said. She fell backward on her bed and reached over to flick on the lamp on her nightstand. "I can't see you, either."

He turned the phone and she saw him sprawled on his back on a big bed with some sort of padded brocade headboard behind him. His shirt was unbuttoned and he had one arm stretched up over his head. He was holding the phone up above him with his other hand.

"Better?"

She sighed. She shouldn't do this late at night when her defenses were down. And they were down. She was feeling mopey and alone. Her mom was due back tomorrow and maybe that would help. But for tonight she had Rafe.

"I miss you."

"You do?"

"I do. You look like you had a formal event tonight," she said. She'd seen him on the news entering a gala with the blonde on his arm earlier this evening.

"I did. Listen, if you saw any pictures on the news of me with a woman, it was just state business. She's nothing to me."

"Does she know that?" Emily asked. Because that woman had seemed as though she had her claws sunk into him.

"Would I be here with you if she didn't?" he asked.

She looked at him in the shadows. "Would you?"

"No. I thought you knew me better than that," he said.

She had made him angry but she needed to know if he was the kind of man who'd cheat on her. "We don't have anything official between us. I...are you a one-woman man?"

He leaned in toward the camera, so close she could see the green and dark brown flecks in his hazel eyes. "I am."

"Then stop having your picture taken with foreign blondes," she said.

He sighed. "It's not that easy. She keeps showing up everywhere I am."

Emily was tempted to go to Alma and—

Do what?

She was Rafe's baby mama, not his fiancée.

This was something she had no idea how to handle. But she wanted him to be hers. For the world to know that he belonged to her. But she didn't want to say that to him. Admit that all these late calls had made her start to fall for him.

"How was your day?" She toed off her socks and grabbed a second pillow to prop her head up.

"Interesting. My baby sister is worried about me."

"Why?"

"She said I don't seem happy," Rafe said.

"Are you?"

"Happy isn't exactly something I aspire to. I think that is a path to crazy," he said. "I'd like to be content."

"Happiness equals crazy?" she asked. "I've never thought that."

"I mean trying to be happy all the time. Life isn't about always being happy. There are quiet moments and the normal grind. That's what makes the happy times memorable."

"So is this a quiet moment?"

"It's so much more than that, Red. You're my reward for being the good son and doing what's expected of me here in Alma."

It wasn't what she wanted to hear, but it warmed her up and made the feelings that had been dogging her all night dissolve. She realized that she'd been edgy and mopey because she didn't like seeing Rafe with that blonde woman.

"I was jealous."

"Of?"

"That blonde." She made a face and put her thumb over the part of her phone that showed her end of the video chat. She didn't want to see her own face.

"Don't be."

"I want this to be light and easy, Rafe. But it's not. It hasn't been for a while."

"You want the truth, Red?" he asked, rolling

to his side and propping his phone up on something so that he wasn't holding it any more.

"You know I do."

"This hasn't been light or easy since the moment I first kissed you. I'm not a one-night-stand guy and we both know you don't take guys home all the time. We've both been trying to pretend that it was nothing more than a moment, but I think it's time we stopped pretending."

She swallowed hard. Had she been pretending? Was that why she'd been jealous and lonely?

"What do you suggest?"

"That we figure out what we both want. I know I want you. Not just for sex."

"Me, too."

Six

It was somehow easier to talk to her when he saw her face. She looked good, with that smattering of freckles across the bridge of her nose and the weary hope in her blue eyes. She seemed to want him to be the man he wasn't sure he could be.

He wanted to be a man of his word, but that was complicated. Making promises to her was out of the question because he had to figure out a solution that would take care of his family's future. Or did he? He was tired of walking on the tightrope between what he wanted and what he should do.

He thought of his mom, who'd divorced their father when Bella turned eighteen. It was as if his mother had served her time raising them and was ready to do something for herself. He didn't want to wait like that… Besides, assuming the throne was for life.

"What are you thinking? You got all intense all of a sudden," Emily said.

"I was thinking about my mom," he admitted quietly. "How she raised us until Bella was eighteen and then moved on with her life. What kind of mom will you be?"

"Not that kind. But I'm independent," she said. "I imagine my child will be too."

"It's our child."

"You're going to be ruling Alma, Rafe. I'm the one who will raise our child."

He didn't like her point. But he knew better than to argue it. He wasn't in a position to win. And he was tired of losing.

"You look nice. No sign of the pregnancy yet," he said.

"Thanks. A Shady Harry's T-shirt and jeans aren't exactly haute couture but they suit me."

They did suit her. He wanted to suit her as well. Be a part of that life. Yet he was torn. How could he be?

"I've got to get changed. I smell like the bar."

"Can I watch?" he asked. Seeing her brought all of his senses into sharp focus and made the life he'd been living these last few days look as if it were in black and white. He had been on autopilot doing what was expected of him and doing it well, but now he truly felt the first spark of excitement...of life.

"Is that what you want?" she asked. There was a teasing note in her voice and he caught a glimpse of the woman who'd bound him with his own shirt in South Beach.

If she only knew the power she wielded over him.

"It is."

"Well okay then," she said. "It's not going to be very exciting. I mean I've never worked in a high-end strip club or anything."

He shook his head. "I didn't think you had."

"Have you been to one?" she asked.

"Are you going to go on a feminist rant if I say yes?" he asked.

"No, I'm not. The women who work in places like that usually earn a good living. And it's their choice to make," she said. "So you have been to one."

He shrugged. Some nights that was where the crowd he ran with back in Miami had ended up. "It's not my favorite place to hang out."

"That's good to know. You should know I've only gotten undressed in front of a few guys."

"You should know I have no interest in any of the other men in your life," he said. "I want to be the only one."

He knew he had no right to say that. That he might not even be able to claim Emily but, hell, this was the twenty-first century and he wasn't going to marry another "suitable" woman when he felt this strongly about her.

She touched her finger to the screen and he

imagined he felt her light touch on his face. "As of right now you are."

She got to her feet and his screen was filled with the image of her ceiling until she got to the bathroom. She flipped on the light switch and she propped the phone up on the counter. "I need a shower, too."

"How about a bath? If I were there, I'd fill that big claw-foot tub of yours with warm water and bubbles and have it waiting for you when you got home."

He wanted to take care of her. She was the first person outside of the circle of his family he'd ever felt this way about.

"Okay. Give me a few minutes."

"Don't take your clothes off until I can see you."

"Do you have a bathtub in your big palace?" she asked. "I saw some pictures of your entire family walking around the gardens on CNN last night. Looked nice."

"I do have a very nice bathroom here. The tub is controlled by a computer," he said.

"Join me in the bath?" she asked. There was a hint of vulnerability in her words. He found it both enchanting and a little bit unnerving. Emily was a very strong woman who didn't really need anyone. But tonight he caught a glimpse behind that attitude and saw that she did need him.

That made him feel like Atlas, strong enough to carry the weight of the earth on his shoulders. And like the mythological being he couldn't simultaneously protect Emily and shoulder his burden. He had no idea where any of this was going. He was used to being the strong one. The one who knew exactly what needed to be done—

And he did this time. He needed to let her go, but for once wanted to be selfish and keep her. For tonight he was going to do just that.

"Okay," he said, getting up and going to his own opulently appointed bathroom. He selected the temperature from a computerized keypad on the wall and soon the water started flowing into the tub. He flicked on the overhead light that just illuminated the tub and then glanced back at his phone screen to see where Emily was.

She was sitting on the edge of her tub biting her lower lip as she fiddled with the taps.

Then she stood up and undid her jeans.

"Hey. Not so fast, Red. I want to see every inch of you," he said.

"Fair enough. Take your shirt off. Not that you don't look sexy with it unbuttoned and your chest showing."

He'd undone his shirt earlier because he felt uncomfortable and hadn't really known what to wear for a video call with her. He lifted his arms. "You see these buttons?"

"Yeah?"

"You're supposed to undo them first. That way I don't have to rip the shirt," he said.

"I like it when you rip your shirt," she said with a wink. "In fact the next time I see you I've got a new shirt for you to try on. One that is made of tougher material."

Arching one eyebrow at her, he tossed his shirt toward the corner and then stood there, feeling a bit ridiculous.

"Damn, you look good," she said.

The open admiration in her eyes as she looked at him made him feel ten feet tall. He rubbed his hand over his chest. And then flexed his muscles for her. He heard her intake of breath. And suddenly all those reps he did at the gym were worth it. He worked out because he lived in South Beach and owned a very successful business. He wasn't about to have a photo of himself looking like a sloth turn up anywhere. But knowing she liked his body gave him another reason to do it.

"Your turn. I want to see your…muscles."

She laughed. "I did help unload a beer delivery this afternoon, so I think my arms are looking a little buffer than usual."

He frowned. "Why are you unloading anything? Harry should know better."

"He does. He was pissed when he got there. But the delivery guys weren't our usual ones and they were piling the beer in the sun…no one else was there. Harry ripped them a new one and they apologized to me."

Good. Still, Rafe didn't like that she'd had to deal with those guys. She should be pampered while she carried his child.

She pulled the Shady Harry's T-shirt up over her head and he immediately noticed her breasts swelling around the sides of the cups of her bra. She reached behind her back and unhooked the bra and let it slid down her arms and onto the floor. Her nipples looked bigger and a darker shade of pink than he remembered. Signs of the changes his baby was having on her body. She skimmed her hand down to her stomach and he noticed just the smallest bump there.

She unhooked her jeans and pushed them down her legs with her panties. And just like that, she was standing there naked.

He touched the image on his phone and realized that seeing her like this was a double-edged sword. He wanted to be there with her.

And that's when he came to his decision. He was going home first thing in the morning. He didn't care what the parliament thought; he needed to be back in Florida with Emily. Even if it was just for a few days.

"Dammit, Red. You get more beautiful each time I see you naked."

She blushed, and he observed that the color started at the top of her breasts and swept up her neck to her cheeks. She shook her head. "I had to unbutton my jeans at work tonight. It's not like they are too tight…well, okay, they are, but it was uncomfortable for the first time."

"I can see the little bump," he said. He traced his finger over her body on the screen. The changes were small, but this was their child making itself known in their lives. Well, mostly hers as of right now. He was missing out.

"I see a little bump in your pants as well," she said with a wink.

He guessed she didn't want to talk about the pregnancy, and he let her change the subject. "Little? Woman, look again."

He undid his pants and carefully shoved them down his legs until he stood there naked. He heard her sharp intake of breath and then her wolf whistle. She was good for his ego. And she kept things light. Was he ever seeing the real woman?

"Not so little."

"Not around you," he said.

"I didn't mean for this to be phone sex," she said.

"I never mean for it to turn into sex with you, but damn, Red, you turn me on like no one else ever has."

She smiled at me. "I feel the same. But I smell like the bar."

"Not to me. To me you smell like Florida sunshine and a day at the beach."

She walked over to the tub with the phone, her heart-shaped face filling the screen. Her eyes were sparkling, and unless he missed his guess, she was happy. While he might not think happiness was a good goal for every second of his life, he was glad to see her smiling.

She propped her phone up on the ledge of the tub and then climbed in. She closed her eyes and let her head fall back against the pillow she had there. The edges of her long hair fell into the water. She looked like his mermaid.

His.

He climbed into his tub, balled a towel up behind his head. The water felt hot and luxurious against his sensitive skin.

"This is nice. But I'm always by myself," she said.

"Me, too."

"Even in that crowd that's always with you?" she asked.

"Yeah."

"If I was there, I'd climb in behind you and rub your shoulders," she said. "You seem stressed."

"I'd like that. But only because I'd feel your naked breasts against my back."

"Maybe I'd lean over you and kiss your neck. Nibble on your earlobe. I know you like that, too."

He stretched his legs to make room for his growing erection and rubbed his hand over his own chest. He wished she were here so he could touch her. But his imagination was doing a good job of filling in the gaps.

"I'd probably pull you around in my arms and kiss you. I can't resist your mouth," he said.

"That's good. I like the way you taste, Rafe. No other guy I've kissed has tasted so right."

Damned straight. He wanted to be the only guy who felt right to her. In all things. A wave of pure possessiveness overwhelmed him and he knew he wanted to claim her as his. But this damned situation with his family was keeping him from doing it.

"I'd put my hands on your waist and lift you up a bit until I could reach your breasts. Are they more sensitive now?"

She nodded.

"Show me."

"How?" she asked. She shifted up on her knees and leaned toward the phone. "I like your mouth on me."

Damn. He did, too. Her nipples felt so right in his mouth, and nothing made him harder than when he swirled his tongue around them and she gripped the back of his head.

"Touch yourself. Run your finger around your nipple and pinch it. Pretend I'm biting you," he said as she shifted back. "Just talking has made your nipples hard."

She nodded and gave him a slow smile. "I've been thinking about you touching me. Remembering how your mouth felt against my nipple."

"Show me," he said again.

She brought her hand up from the water, the droplets sparkling in the light as they fell from her arm. Then she cupped her breast and trailed her finger around her nipple. It puckered as she touched it, and he got even harder watching her as her head fell back and she let out a moan.

"Feel good?" he asked, his voice husky and low. His skin was so sensitive that each lap of the water brought him closer to the edge. He was going to come. But he didn't want to until she did. He wanted to keep watching her for as long as he could. And draw out the pleasure so he could feel as if they were together. He needed this. Needed her.

He'd been trying to deny it, but there it was. The truth that he'd been afraid to admit to himself.

She was cupping both of her breasts and he groaned as he reached for the screen of his phone and touched it. He remembered the way she felt underneath him. How her limbs felt wrapped around his.

"Not as good as when you do touch me," she said. "If I were there I'd caress your chest and then slowly tease you by working my fingers lower."

"When you do that it makes it difficult for me to think," he admitted.

"Really?"

He nodded. Words were sort of beyond him at this moment.

"Are you hard for me?" she asked.

"I am." He stroked himself, remembering how she fit him like a glove when he thrust into her.

"Show me," she said. "Let me see how hard you are."

Her words were like a velvet lash on his skin and he shuddered. This was excruciating. He wanted to come inside her and each time she said something so sexual he couldn't contain his groans.

"Red…"

"Show me, Rafe. I want to see you. See how much you want me."

He groaned, but did as she asked, shifting until he was out of the water and she could see him. He stroked his hand up and down his shaft.

"Swipe your finger over the top," she said. "Pretend it's my tongue on you."

He did as she instructed and then shuddered as he realized how close to the edge he was.

"Are you ready for me? Show me," he said.

She parted her legs and showed him. Pushed her finger up inside and moaned as she did so. "It's not the same as when you do it."

"Does it feel good?" he asked.

"It does."

"Come for me, Red."

This was too intimate and yet not intimate enough.

"I want to touch you, Rafe. If I were there I'd take you inside me. I need you," she said.

"Me, too, Red."

She moaned. "I'm so ready for it. For you."

He was, too. He remembered the way it had felt the last time they were together. How she'd gripped him as soon as he entered her body. How deep he'd gone and the way her eyes had opened and he'd met her gaze. Felt her wrapped around him all the way to his soul.

"Rafe."

Hearing her name on his lips made him come. He closed his eyes and put his head back as his orgasm washed over him. He opened them to see her doing the same. She gave him a slow, sexy smile.

"That's my kind of bath," she said, smiling.

"Mine, too," he said. "When I get home I want to do this again."

"But together in the same tub."

He hit the button to drain the tub and got to his feet. She stayed where she was, watching him, and he realized that in her eyes he was enough. He didn't have to prove anything to her. Or at least he hoped he didn't have to. Because he was coming to realize he didn't know who he was anymore. He hadn't known in a long, long time.

"Come to bed with me, Red. Let's talk until we both fall asleep."

She nodded. She got out of the tub and dried herself off and he just watched, absently toweling himself dry. He caught his breath when she padded naked back to her bed and climbed between the sheets. She'd washed the sheets but not the pillow case he'd slept on.

"This pillow smells like you," she said.

"It does?"

"Yes. I've been pretending you are here with me every night… Tomorrow I'm going to deny that. But tonight I need you here with me."

He understood. When the sun was out there were oceans between them and problems that wouldn't be easily solved. And while he wanted to do what Bella said and put himself first—maybe marry Emily so that the rest of the world would have to accept her—he knew she wouldn't go for that. She didn't want a man who could be hers only halfway.

And that was all he could offer right now. But he knew he wanted to call her his and he needed to figure out a way.

He climbed into his own bed and curled on his side. "I don't have a pillow that smells like you."

"Sorry, babe."

She smiled sleepily at him and he watched her as she started to drift off to sleep. "Thank you for being here tonight."

"You're welcome, Red."

He watched over her until he knew she was sound asleep and snoring slightly. Maybe he kept the line open for longer than he should have before disconnecting the call.

He knew he couldn't do this any longer. He was tired of making do with phone calls to Emily. He'd thought that the video call would make it easier but it hadn't. Instead it made him long to touch her. Really touch her.

He got out of his bed, pacing to the window and looking out at the sea. The ocean was endless and as he glanced up at the moon that was almost setting he realized that in Emily's part of the world the moon was rising. He wanted to be in the same place she was. See if there was anything really between them.

Honestly he knew this wasn't real. How could it be? He was painting her the way he wanted her to be. And not to be oedipal or anything, but he was making Emily into the woman he wanted while imagining her as the mother he never had.

He got dressed and walked out of his room down the hall to Gabe's. He figured Gabe would be easier to talk to than Juan Carlos. But there was no answer when he knocked.

He rubbed the back of his neck.

Damn.

He walked to Juan Carlos's room and wasn't surprised when his cousin answered the door wearing a dressing gown with the Alma royal seal monogramed on the breast.

"What is it?"

"I…I have to return to the States."

"Why? You know that royal protocol states—"

"Screw royal protocol, J.C. I had a life before Alma came to us and I can't just walk away from it."

"You gave your word. Our family gave our word. You are the oldest."

"I wish I wasn't."

"Stop being so selfish. This country needs a leader. It needs someone who can take it from the isolated kingdom it's been into the twenty-first century. You are the man."

"I didn't choose this," Rafe said. "I'm not sure I want this."

"Too bad, Rafael, you're birthright has brought you to this. Sure, it would have been easier if we'd been brought up on the island but that doesn't make our legacy any less important."

Juan Carlos would be so much better at this

than him, Rafe thought. But he wasn't from the right family line and Rafe really couldn't—

"I have to return to the States," he said again. "I'm the one who will be king so my decision is final."

"This is ridiculous."

"Why?"

"Because already I can see that your loyalty isn't to your people. And they will see it too."

"I can't take care of the people of Alma until I figure out this part of my life."

"Is there a woman?"

"Yes. Yes, there is, and I haven't had a chance to resolve anything with her."

"Is she…would the court approve a marriage to her?"

Rafe doubted it. Hell, he wasn't even sure he wanted to marry her. He had to get back to her and figure this all out.

"I have no idea if I want to marry her or not. I need some time to myself to figure this out."

"Hell. I'll go with you."

"I don't want the entire family to know," Rafe said. "Why would you come with me?"

"As you said, you can't be a good ruler until you know where you belong. I want that, Rafe. I know I seem all tied up with royal protocol, but I want what is best for all of us. You're like a brother to me."

"You are to me as well," Rafe said. Juan Carlos had grown up in their home after his parents had died. "I do need to be in Miami to take care of the details of the new shipping deal I just signed. I will let the court and the coronation committee know that's why I'm returning."

"I will back you up," Juan Carlos said. "Just be sure you make the right decision."

Rafe nodded. His impromptu decision to leave had to be delayed until he could talk to the court advisors and his family. Since it was early morning it would take time for the entire Montoro clan who were in Alma to be ready to go.

But sure enough, later that day, they were all on the plane and headed toward Miami.

Seven

Emily went to Key Koffee for a cup of decaf and sat at the corner table again. Last night with Rafe had been different. It had been fun, but also, in the safety of the darkness and with the distance between them, she felt he'd shared more of himself than he had before.

Caution, she warned herself.

Her mom was always warning her about racing headlong into action before thinking about it first. But she felt as if it was too late to change. And last night had made her fall a little more for Rafe.

Which was probably why she was up early

even though she had to work later. But her mom was also due to dock at the marina at nine, and Emily wanted to be there to greet her.

"Give me a double espresso and a lemon poppy-seed muffin to go as well as my usual order," Emily said to Cara behind the bar.

"Sure thing. Feeling hungry this morning?"

"A little, but the extra stuff is for my mom. She's back in port today," she told Cara.

"How about your man?" Cara asked.

Emily shook her head. "I don't have a man."

She couldn't claim Rafe as her own until he indicated he was ready for that. And she knew despite their closeness when they were alone that he wasn't. That knowledge sort of tinged her day. She frowned a little. The smell of the espresso was strong this morning, and she felt bile rising in the back of her throat.

She swallowed hard to keep from getting sick and then realized it wasn't going to work. She ran for the bathroom but made it only as far as the hallway before she began retching. She forced herself to keep moving into the bathroom and threw up. She was heavy and aching and knew this wasn't one of the times when she could say she was enjoying her pregnancy.

Cara followed her into the bathroom with a wet towel. After Emily rinsed her mouth and splashed water on her face, Cara walked her back to her table. Emily felt as if everyone was staring at her. Cara just smiled at them.

"She's pregnant. You don't worry about our food."

Everyone nodded and went back to their papers and electronic devices.

"I sort of wasn't planning on telling anyone yet," Emily said.

"Sorry, Em. But I can't have people thinking it's my food."

"It's okay," Emily said.

"Your man should be here with you," Cara said in a kind way. "I saw you two together. He's not the kind of man who'd just walk away."

Cara tucked a strand of Emily's hair behind her ear. "Have you told him?"

She wasn't that close to Cara, but they were

friends. They'd gone to the same high school and had even taken a road trip to Georgia together one time. But she didn't want to discuss Rafe with her. "Yes. It's complicated."

"Fair enough. Park yourself right there. I'm going to get your order for you."

Emily looked up and noticed a man watching her. The same guy who had been eavesdropping on her telephone conversation with Rafe the other day.

"How you feeling?" he asked, coming over with a packet of Club crackers that they kept on the tables for when Key Koffee serve conch chowder in the afternoon. "These always helped my wife when she was expecting."

She smiled her thanks and took them, weakly opening the pack and taking out a cracker. She munched on one and tipped her head back as her body stopped rioting and started to calm down.

"Are you reading this?" he asked.

She glanced down at the *Miami Herald,* which

was flipped open to the society page with a picture of Rafe and his family in Alma.

"No."

"I can't believe how obsessed everyone is with that family," the guy said. "I'm Stan, by the way."

"Emily," she said. "Well, it's a fairy tale, isn't it? American royalty becomes real royalty."

"True enough. I've heard that Rafe comes down to Key West," Stan said.

It seemed to her that he was fishing for information. She didn't know if he was some obsessed royal watcher or just making conversation. "I guess he does. It's not that uncommon."

"No it's not. But surely now that he's going to be king he won't be," Stan added.

"I have no idea," Emily admitted.

"Mind if I take this paper?"

"Be my guest," she said.

"Thanks," he said, walking out.

"Here's your breakfast to go," Cara said, coming over. "What did he want?"

"The newspaper," Emily said. She started to get up but Cara pushed her back down. "Sit for a little while. I called Harry to come and get you."

"Cara."

"What? You're family, Em. We take care of our own here," she reminded her.

She felt tears burn the back of her eyes and blinked so they didn't fall. She'd always felt as if Key West was her home, ever since she was three years old and her mother moved them there. The people she knew were like family to her, but she had always figured it was a one-way street. The feelings of a girl left too many times by a mother whose job was her life, her obsession.

"Thanks, Cara. But I'm a big girl."

"Even big girls deserve to be looked after," Harry said, walking into the coffee shop and approaching their table. "We got time for me to grab a cup of coffee?"

"No need to wait, Harry," Cara said, handing him a cup and a bakery bag.

Unless Emily missed her guess, that bakery bag would have a toasted everything bagel in it. Cara was right. They were all family.

This place was as much a part of her as the baby growing inside her. And though she didn't need the reassurance, it was nice to know that she wasn't alone. That if Rafe made the choice that any sane man would and took the throne of Alma half a world away from her, she'd still have family around her. Her baby would grow up with the family she'd chosen for herself and not the one she'd been born into. The family her mother had chosen for them when she'd moved them to Key West.

"You okay, kiddo?" Harry asked.

"Just morning sickness."

"Another thing that I will bring up to Rafe Montoro the next time he shows his face here."

Rafe stretched his long legs out in front of him as he settled in for the flight. His cousin Juan Carlos—the one in the family who was the best suited for royal life since he seemed to know so much about it—sat across from him reading a book on the history of Alma from the 1970s to today.

His father, brother and sister were all sitting in the back of the plane talking quietly amongst themselves. They were happy enough to follow his lead especially when he mentioned that the oil deal needed his attention in Miami.

Rafe had been surprised by Juan Carlos's understanding but now he realized he shouldn't have been. He knew his cousin as well as he knew Gabe...though he had to admit that he'd known both men better when they were children. But the bond among all of them was still strong. And Rafe felt less isolated that he had before. Felt a little more as if his family had his back.

Rafe read the book last week, since the government people wanted to make sure that everyone in the Montoro camp was familiar with the past. The common consensus being that maybe then they wouldn't make the same mistakes again. Rafe didn't want to have to flee the country in the middle of the night and start over with nothing.

At least his great-grandfather had his wife by his side, and his family. Something that was becoming more and more important to Rafe.

"Juan, what would you do if you were going to be king?" Rafe asked. "I'm tempted to invest Montoro Enterprises money into the manufacturing sector so that Alma isn't just reliant on oil."

"That's a start. They really need stability so that Alma's citizens will start staying on the island instead of emigrating to countries in the EU. I think we should try to become a member of the EU as well," Juan Carlos said.

"It's one of the prime minister's top priorities. He has me scheduled to go to Brussels next month for meetings on the subject," Rafe said, rubbing the back of his neck.

"I can go with you if you like," Juan Carlos said. "I'm not as impatient as you are at the negotiating table. Of course, you are always very shrewd at getting the best deal for Montoro Enterprises."

"That would be great. I'd love to have you there with me," Rafe said. One thing about his family that had been made clear during the last few weeks as they'd traveled to Alma and gotten a handle on their new lives was how they all banded together. "When is Tia Isabella going to join us in Alma?"

"Soon, I hope," Juan Carlos said. Juan Carlos's grandmother suffered from Parkinson's and had her good days and her bad days. "We are waiting for her doctors to okay the visit."

"How is she doing?" Rafe asked. "You talk to her nurse every day, don't you?"

"Yes, I do. I think the thought of returning to Alma has rallied her spirits, and though medically I'd have to say there have been no changes, she seems healthier."

Rafe smiled to himself. The very thing that felt like a burden to him was a dream come true to Tia Isabella. She had longed to return to her home for decades and now it was possible.

That almost made his royal sacrifice worthwhile. But there was also a lot to be said for the old-world charm of Playa del Onda. And for Juan Carlos's excitement over their all being part of the royal aristocracy again as well.

It just made everything more difficult for Rafe. He wanted to keep his family happy. He was the eldest and had the power to do it. But then he remembered Emily and he was torn.

Had been torn for too long. When he got to Miami he needed to see her and figure this entire thing out.

"Do you think that the government would accept a commoner as my wife?" Rafe asked his cousin. They were still negotiating the constitution that Alma's parliament had brought to them. Rafe had been asking for little changes because he wanted to see how far they would go to get him and his family back in the country.

"Is your woman a commoner?" Juan Carlos asked.

"Not many royals in the States, Juan Carlos." He didn't want to talk about Emily with anyone else. Not yet. Why then did he keep bringing her up? He clearly needed to talk even if he didn't want to. Not until he had her sorted out. God, she'd kill him if she knew he thought that way about her.

"I don't know. I think they want you to marry a woman who will reinforce the monarchy, and a commoner wouldn't do that," Juan Carlos said at last.

Rafe nodded at his cousin and then leaned back and closed his eyes. He'd figured as much. There was no way to have it both ways. Why was he still trying to?

Because he couldn't walk away from Emily.

There it was: the truth he'd been trying to pretend didn't exist for too long. And letting his family down, well, that wasn't something he was prepared to do, either. He wasn't even sure if he walked away from the throne that they would let him keep his job at Montoro Enterprises. Though truth be told, he was a genius at making money, so he had no doubt he could start his own company and make it a success.

But that would mean walking away from everything and everyone. His family was so deeply rooted in his life, he truly wasn't sure what he'd do without them. When they'd lived in the Miami area, he saw them every day at their Coral Gables compound. He worked hard for all of them so that they wouldn't have to worry.

That was why he hesitated. Then there was Tia Isabella. With her deteriorating health, Rafe didn't really want to do anything to upset her. If he walked away, would he find a way to make peace with the family before her illness got the better of her? Bella would be forced into a difficult position as well. His father would more than likely try to come between her and Rafe, and that would cause her stress. She liked to keep the peace.

Gabriel would be none too pleased with him. Gabe lived a nice and easy lifestyle, enjoying the many beautiful women who flocked to Miami. No-strings relationships were his MO.

Rafe laughed to himself. Gabe always did whatever the hell he wanted. He'd be plenty pissed at Rafe if he walked away from the throne and Gabe had to take it. That would be a nightmare for all concerned. His younger brother was a player. Not the image that Alma wanted for their new king.

So Rafe was back to the exact same position he'd been in since he left Miami. Except this time he was leaning more toward Emily. Hell, last night had changed something between them.

He no longer saw her as the fun-loving bartender who had gotten pregnant, but more as Emily, the woman who was going to be the mother to their child.

Their child. If he had a son he'd be Rafael V. Or would he? Would Emily want to name him something else? There was still so much for them to discuss.

He closed his eyes, trying to picture what their child would look like. Would the baby have his dark hair and eyes or Emily's bright blue ones? He tried to picture the little tyke, maybe with her red hair and his hazel eyes.

He wanted to be a part of that. Be a part of

his child's life. He had to find a way to have it all. Perhaps he needed introduce Emily to his family so they could start to get to know her. Once that happened, they would be on his side. And marrying a commoner wouldn't be such a big issue.

At first Emily might be reluctant about this plan of action, but Rafe was confident he could change her mind and bring her around to his way of thinking.

He'd seen that look in her eyes as she'd drifted off to sleep last night. She cared for him. He was gambling that she wanted him in her life as much as he wanted to be there.

He'd never been much of a gambling man. He preferred to take risks where he could control the outcome. But there was no controlling Em. She was a force unto herself and no matter what happened, she was never going to be coerced into doing anything she wasn't comfortable with.

Emily, her mom and Harry spent a pleasant day together at her house. It was nice to forget about everything and just enjoy having her mom home.

Jessica Fielding had the same blue eyes as Emily but her hair was blond and cut short in a low-maintenance bob. She'd had a look of mild concern on her face ever since she docked earlier today. "So how far along are you?" she asked.

"About eight weeks. I'm not really showing yet but have lots of morning sickness," Emily said as her mom got up and brought her a glass of homemade lemonade and a gingersnap. Emily had been ordered to sit on the padded chaise longue in the shade of a big magnolia tree in the backyard while Harry manned the grill preparing fish for their dinner and her mom bustled around doing things for Emily that she could do herself.

She'd protested at first, but then figured her mom was only in town for a few days and it was okay to let her spoil her. Well, fetching drinks and fixing dinner was probably going to be the extent of the spoiling. Her mom wasn't one of those in-your-face, hands-on parents.

"Tell me about the father," her mom said. "Is he totally out of the picture?"

Emily took a sip of her lemonade. "Not entirely. Was my dad when you were pregnant?"

"Em," Jessica said.

"Mom, I want to know more about him. I'm not going to suddenly show up on his doorstep—how could I? Is he even alive?" These were the questions she'd kept hidden away for years but the truth was, she needed to know now more than ever. She'd always wanted to know for herself but really felt as if she had to know the answers to share with your child.

"No, you can't show up on his doorstep, Emily. He's dead. He died when you were three," Jessica said at last. She rubbed her hand over her forehead and Emily almost felt bad for asking about him.

But she had a right to know. Someday her child was going to want to know about Rafe, and Emily planned to have the answers ready.

"Why didn't you ever tell me this?"

"You never asked."

"I didn't ask because you seemed sad whenever I said anything about my father," Emily said.

"Sorry, sweetie, I just thought you were too young to understand and then as you got older you never brought it up so I kept quiet."

"Is that why we moved here?" Emily asked.

"That was part of it. Also, I had the grant so I needed to live someplace where I could do my work and be home every night for you," Jessica said

She got that. Work had always been her mother's driving force. Emily had been swimming before she learned to walk and had understood boat safety by the time she was six. Her life had been on the water and as an assistant to her mother's work. The work always came first, and Em had understood that at a very early age.

Emily was beginning to think of what she would do once her baby was born, and though she hadn't talked to Harry yet, she was pretty sure she wouldn't be tending bar.

"Did he want me?" Emily asked. It was the question that had weighed on her mind for a long time.

"He did, sweetie, but he had another family. He was a married man," Jessica said at last. "He saw you from time to time before he died. But really he knew that he couldn't leave his wife."

That wasn't what she'd expected. A married man. Had her mother known he was married? It didn't fit the picture she had of her mother, of the woman she'd always thought her mother was. Then the thought struck her that she might have another family.

"Do I have siblings?" she asked, mildly alarmed by the thought of strangers who might share her DNA.

"No. His wife was infertile and they never had children. He offered to adopt you and raise you with his wife, but I couldn't let you go."

Harry left his position by the grill and went over to her mother, putting his hand on her shoulder. Emily realized now why her mom had never spoken of her father. But she was glad to finally know something about him.

She went over to her mom and hugged her tightly. Her mom hugged her back, and then kissed the top of her head.

"I love you, Mom."

"I love you too, honey. I'm sorry I never talked about him."

"It's okay," Emily said. "Thank you."

"For what?" she asked, tucking a strand of hair behind Emily's ear.

"Telling me. I hated not knowing. I always felt… Well, that doesn't matter now," Emily said. But she'd always felt an emptiness inside her where a father should be. Now she knew. Their situation had been complicated. More so than her own?

She wasn't too sure.

"Tell me about the father of your child," Jessica said.

"He's Rafael Montoro IV," Emily said. Then she realized that she always used his full name when she told people about him so they'd get why he wasn't with her. She was sort of making excuses for coming second in his life. "We had a weekend together and then I got pregnant. His family got called back to Alma to restore the monarchy before I knew I was going to have his baby."

"Harry filled me in on a few of the details via our calls on the satellite phone."

Jessica sat down on the end of the chaise longue and lifted Emily's legs, drawing them over her lap. "Well, I can see why you said it was complicated. What did he say when you told him about the baby?"

"I caught him on his way out of town, Mom. We really didn't have any time to talk. I wanted him to know he had a kid coming but I never expected anything from him."

Her mom nodded. "You're strong enough to raise the baby on your own, and you have me."

"And me," Harry said.

Emily smiled over at Harry. "I know. But I think he wants to be a part of the baby's life."

"And yours?"

She bit her lower lip. She'd been telling herself that he did, but what if she was just seeing something that wasn't there? Emotions and bonds that she wanted to see because she'd started to care about him. And not just because he was her baby's father.

"I don't know. He's been calling me every day while he's in Alma. He sent me that beautiful mermaid that's hanging in the kitchen."

Her mom smiled. "Remember when you wanted to be a mermaid?"

She nodded.

"You told him?" her mom asked. "Oh, baby, I'd hoped you wouldn't fall for a man who wasn't available."

She had, too. Of course until this afternoon she'd had no idea how much her own life might parallel her mother's, but it was clear now that the Fielding women always seemed to go for men who were already spoken for.

"I'm not sure I've fallen for him."

"You are starting to," her mom said.

"Mom." Her mom always had to push her when she wasn't ready.

"Dinner's ready, ladies," Harry said, interrupting the fight that he could sense brewing.

They went to the table and Harry served the fish her mom had caught that morning and fresh mango with grilled green onions. It was delicious and Emily forgot her ire at her mother as they finished eating.

This was turning out to be one of the best days she'd had in a while. She'd talked to Rafe this morning and felt closer to him than ever. She'd learned the details of her own parentage and felt closer to her mom than ever before.

Her mom picked up the dishes and went into the kitchen to watch the evening weather forecast, something she did every night so she'd know what to expect on the water the next day.

"You better come in here and see this," her mom said as she leaned out the window.

Emily got to her feet, looking up at the evening summer sky and wondering if it looked similar in Alma.

She stepped inside and noticed that that instead of the local fishing report the television was tuned to E! News. She'd been watching *Keeping up with the Kardashians* earlier. Now the words *Montoro Baby Mama!* were on the screen and Emily felt as if she was going to be sick.

Eight

Rafe turned his phone to flight-safe mode once they were getting ready to land. There was a tingle of excitement in the pit of his stomach as he made plans to bring Emily to his family. She was stubborn, so he knew it wouldn't be easy to convince her to leave Key West, but he was fairly confident that he had his ways of persuading her.

They landed at the private airfield the Montoros always used. As Rafe got off the plane and started walking across the tarmac, he noticed there seemed to be a swarm of reporters waiting. Had something happened in Alma in the last ten hours while he'd been on the plane? He slowed down, as did the rest of the party, all looking at one another as they flicked on their phones and scanned headlines.

Gabe was the first one to spot it and cursed under his breath.

"Your baby mama is headline news," Gabe said.

His baby mama.

Damn.

"It's not like that," he said.

Juan Carlos looked pissed but he was quiet as he simply turned away from Rafe and walked toward the hangar. He couldn't have known that the press would find out about Emily while they were in the air. Rafe shoved his hands into his pockets and rocked back on his heels.

Gabe clapped a sympathetic hand on his shoulders before following the rest of their party into the hangar. Rafe's phone finally connected and he saw he had a dozen missed calls from Emily along with seven text messages that all said the same thing. Call me.

She'd already seen the news.

Of course she had. For a brief moment he wondered if she'd leaked the news, but then he remembered how fierce she was about keeping to herself. It was doubtful that she'd rat herself out.

When Rafe got into the hangar, Gabe immediately introduced him to a tall, dapper man in a white linen suit. Geoff Standings was a British press agent who'd once worked for the British royal family. Apparently he'd been sent by the royal advisers back in Alma to meet Rafe's plane and start doing damage control.

Gabe didn't look as amused as he had a few minutes ago.

"We need to fix this," Gabe said.

"Duh."

"No, I mean if the people of Alma decide that you are too hot to touch, then I'm going to have to take your place as king. We need to fix this. Now."

"Fine. Geoff, what do you recommend? I have been planning to introduce Emily to the family, and was even thinking of having a dinner next week where she could meet the members of my family who came with me on the trip. Do you think we should get engaged? Should I marry her?"

"Well, marriage usually is the right step for an illegitimate baby. But in your case I'm going to have to figure this out. I have already sent my assistant to start researching her lineage. Maybe we can find a relation—however distant—to a royal somewhere."

"If that doesn't work?" Rafe asked.

"I think we can make a case for you as a love match. Prince William married a commoner and perhaps Alma won't mind so much if we can make her into a style icon the way Kate is."

Style icon? Rafe doubted Emily would go for that. He loved her style but it was bohemian and beachy. Not exactly what Geoff was talking about.

Geoff was frantically typing away on his smartphone. "Either way, I'm going to book you some shows so you can get out there. Yes, you need to be engaged to her. I'd like to send a press release out that says she's your fiancée, not just your 'baby mama.' Who do you think leaked this?"

Good question.

"I have to ask her before you say she's my fiancée. She might get stubborn if she sees that online or in a paper before I ask," Rafe said.

"Fair enough. Any ideas on the leak?"

"None," Rafe said. "I think she's told her mom and her boss and that's it. Neither of them would tell a reporter."

"Let me look into it and see if I can find out where the information came from. Where will you be?"

"Key West. You've got my cell number, and here is Jose's as well. He's my assistant based at Montoro Enterprises headquarters in Miami and he's at your service."

Juan Carlos returned. "I'll take the family out the front of the airport. I've had your car brought around. Resolve this, Rafe. This needs to be made right."

"I know," he said. "I'll be back in the office in a couple of days to take care of the details of the Alma shipping deal, but I need to go to Key West."

He didn't like answering to his cousin and normally wouldn't have but if Juan Carlos was upset Rafe knew the court advisors in Alma would be as well.

"I was trying to keep this under control," Rafe said.

"I realize that. That's why I'm going to help you as much as I can. Alma needs the Montoros back on the throne."

Juan Carlos gathered the rest of their family. Bella gave Rafe a hug and Gabe shook his head but clapped him on the shoulder before they headed toward the main airport area and the waiting reporters.

No one said another word as Rafe strode out of the airport to his waiting Audi. His phone rang as soon as he was inside. He synched it to Bluetooth and hit the button to answer it.

"Jose here. Have you seen the news? I'm getting calls from morning news shows asking you to come on and tell your story. What should I do?" Jose asked.

"Coordinate with Geoff. He's the PR expert that the Alma court hired to make the scandal go away. I need some media prepared and he's the expert. They are all going nuts over this. Any idea where the leak came from?"

"No, sir. She wasn't visibly pregnant when I delivered your gift and I didn't see any reporters hanging around her place."

"Thanks, Jose. I'm going to leave the phone off while I drive to Key West.

"Why don't you take the chopper? I already have it ready and waiting at the Coral Gables compound."

"I'm trying to decide if I need more time alone to clear my head," he said.

"It's up to you, sir."

If he took the chopper he'd cut his travel time in half and be at Emily's side that much sooner. But he was still not sure what he was going to say when he got there. The plans he'd been hatching as he flew back from Alma were all moot now. He was in damage control, and so was the rest of the family.

"I'll take the chopper."

"I'm turning around and will be in Coral Gables with your bag in a few minutes."

"Where were you headed?"

"Key West," Jose said. "I also have procured two jewelers to meet you. They are waiting in Coral Gables."

"Thanks, Jose." Rafe disconnected the call.

Jose had thought of everything, which was why Rafe paid him the big bucks. Still, Rafe was uncertain. Having the chopper and his bag and even a ring might make going to Key West easier for him, but he had no idea what kind of reception he was going to get when he saw Emily. How was he going to tell her that they had to be engaged? He knew he needed to have that conversation in person and not over the phone. In fact, the sooner he could get to her the better. He needed to think about what he was going to do.

With Em he tended to react first and then do damage control later. This was one time when he needed to plan with his head and not his groin. He wanted her, but he needed the details to be right. There was no more choosing between the throne and Emily.

What kind of king would the people of Alma think he was if he abandoned his child? In a way it was the perfect solution to the debate he'd been having with himself. There was no more keeping Emily and the baby hidden.

Emily gave up trying to call Rafe and convinced her mom and Harry to go home around 11:00 p.m. She changed into a big T-shirt she'd gotten during the last hurricane to hit the Keys with the slogan It Takes More Than a Little Breeze to Shake Me on it.

Harry had called his buddies at the Key West Police Department and together they'd cleared the reporters from her yard and were keeping them at the end of the street. She'd heard a chopper fly over and hadn't turned on the local news because she was afraid she'd see her home on it.

She felt as if this story about being Rafe's "baby mama" was enough to shake her though. She had an idea that the source might be that creepy guy from the coffee shop who'd watched her and made awkward conversation with her. But how had he known about Rafe?

Not that they'd done much to keep it secret. They had been flirting at the bar that weekend he'd been on Key West. Everyone had seen them together. She guessed it wouldn't take Sherlock Holmes to figure out that she and Rafe had hooked up.

But baby mama? That was insulting. She guessed it was meant to be. If it was that creep from the coffee shop, did that rat bastard have a vendetta against Rafe? She vowed to get to the bottom of it tomorrow. She rolled to her side feeling very alone as she stared out the window.

She'd done everything to pretend that it was normal. That she wasn't bothered by the fact that he hadn't called her back.

Why hadn't he?

Surely he knew she hadn't gone to the papers. Didn't he?

There was nothing in it for her if she did. Or maybe he hadn't heard about it yet. But that seemed far-fetched to her, even if she wanted it to be true.

What if he'd decided he'd had enough and the paparazzi were the last straw? It didn't seem like the man she knew to just retreat. More than likely he was coming up with some plan. Maybe he'd ask her and the baby to leave town. Disappear for a while so he could get on with his coronation plans.

Tired of listening to her own thoughts, she got out of bed and wandered through her empty house to the kitchen. She found the carton of frozen yogurt she'd shoved into the back of the freezer when she got home from the grocery store earlier. She'd been trying to hide it from herself because the last time she'd opened a pint of the key lime pie flavor, she'd eaten it in one sitting.

But if ever she needed the cold comfort of fro-yo, it was tonight.

She didn't want to leave Key West, to start over on her own. But she wasn't alone, was she? She had this little pod in her belly.

She dipped her spoon into the carton and took a big scoop, putting it in her mouth as she leaned against the counter. Letting the frozen dessert melt on her tongue was bliss.

She didn't care what was happening outside her little cottage. She'd just stay here with her fro-yo until she figured out how to fix this.

She'd never met a problem she couldn't solve. It was just late-night loneliness making her feel blue. That and the fact that she was getting total radio silence from Rafe. Why didn't he return her call?

She had a feeling this was going to be one of those nights when sleep evaded her. Part of it she blamed on the habits formed by spending her entire adult life working nights, but the other part was worry. She never admitted she was scared. But she was very afraid that this thing with the news might have helped Rafe decide he didn't need her or their baby in his life.

She wasn't thinking that because he was a jerk or anything. It was just that she understood that royals, especially those in a volatile newly reestablished monarchy, probably needed to be above reproach.

Her mind went to the video chat they'd had two nights ago. He hadn't exactly been staid on that call. She guessed that was what appealed to her about him.

She rubbed her stomach as she walked into the living room. Without turning on the lights, she went to her couch and turned on the television and the DVR to watch her comfort movie. But there was a knock on her door before the opening credits started to roll. She paused it and put her frozen yogurt container on the coffee table, grabbing her baseball bat from the hall closet before she went to the front door.

She pushed aside the curtain on the small, narrow window next to the door and peeked out, not sure what she'd find.

Rafe.

Illuminated by her front porch light, he stood there in faded jeans that fit in all the right places and a T-shirt that molded to his chest like a second skin. Not very regal tonight, was he. Very American and very real, though, she thought.

She unlatched the door and let it swing open, keeping her bat in one hand.

"Rafe."

Was he really here?

"Red. Planning to hit me with that bat?" he asked, pulling her into his arms and hugging her tightly. "I'm sorry I didn't return your calls."

"Why didn't you? When did you get back to the States?" she asked. She felt shell-shocked after everything that had been going on this evening. She hated to admit it but she was very glad to see him.

"No. The bat is not for you. I thought if I found that rat bastard reporter snooping around I might take it to him. I was afraid he might have slipped past the patrolmen."

"We don't need it tonight," he said. "Can I come in?"

She stood there feeling a little aggrieved now that she knew he wasn't a threat. That Rafe was here.

"How long have you been back in the States?"

"I got in this afternoon, right about the time the baby story broke," he said.

"And you came here? But not straight here," she said. "It doesn't take that long to get here and I know you've got a helicopter."

"Can we do this inside?" he asked.

She felt the need in him to get his own way but she wasn't threatened by him at all. She stepped back and he walked in, closing the door and leaning back against it. First thing he did was take the bat and drop it on the floor. Then he lifted her off her feet with his hands on her waist.

"I missed you, Red," he said, lowering his mouth to hers and taking a kiss that left no doubt that he wasn't going to walk away from her. She had no idea what he thought their future would be, but she realized as she wrapped her arms around his shoulders that she wanted him by her side.

Rafe took his first deep breath since he'd stepped off the plane in Miami. He was with Em, and right now that was enough. His family, who had always been his stalwart supporters, weren't really there for him now. He tucked that away for further analysis later. He knew it was important, but right now he needed to figure out this threat and convince Emily that his plan to move forward was the best one.

"I thought coming home to you was going to be the first peace I've felt in a few days," he said as he lifted his head and stepped back from her.

"I didn't realize you were coming back to me," she said.

"Are you kidding me? I've been calling you every day. What else did you think that meant?"

She bit her lower lip, reaching behind him to bolt the door before picking up her baseball bat and leaning it against the wall. "I didn't know."

She walked down the hallway lit only by little nightlights plugged into the wall sockets, and he followed her.

All this time he'd thought he was courting her…wait a minute. Was that what he'd been doing?

Yes.

No matter how he'd tried to rationalize it, that was exactly what he'd been doing.

"That's my bad. I was trying to be cool and see if you liked me," he said as he entered her living room. The television projected a soft blue glow into the room and he noted the opened container of frozen yogurt on the coffee table.

She sat in the chair that he had fond memories of making love to her in, with her legs curled under her body. With a quick economical movement she reached over and flicked on the light on the side table.

"I think we both know I *like* you," she said.

He sat down on the ottoman in front of her and put his hands on the arms of the chair. "I'm not talking about lust. I'm talking about whether you like me for the man I am. I don't think I did much but show off the last time I was in Key West. Trying to catch your eye and show you I wasn't like all the other men in the bar."

"You did that," she said softly. "If that was you showing off, you did it very well."

He winked at her. "After all this time I do know how to present a good image."

"It worked. So is that what you were doing in Alma with the people? I saw some of the press coverage from your trip. It looks like you were falling in love with the country and the people."

"You're talking about the blonde, right?" He laughed softly when she frowned and shook her head in denial. "Her family is nuts. They want her to marry the next king. She's not…real. It's not like when I'm with you," he said. Dita was a beautiful woman, but all the scheming with her mother made him edgy. And it was impossible to think of anything other than getting away from her.

"So what do you want from me?" Emily asked.

There it was. The million-dollar question. He

had been debating it for so long and still had no answer. "Right now, I need to figure out how the media found out you were pregnant."

She nodded. "The easy stuff first."

It was interesting that she thought finding the source of the leak was going to be easy. "How is that the easy stuff? Do you know who broke the story?"

"Let's just say I have some suspicions, and if that little weasel is at the coffee shop tomorrow morning I intend to confirm them," she said. "I pretty much caught some guy eavesdropping on me when you and I were talking on the phone the other day. And yesterday...I had really bad bout of morning sickness at the coffee shop and Snoopy was right there talking to me about you. Seems odd, right?"

Rafe didn't like the idea that Emily had been targeted. How had the reporter been alerted to her presence? The community in Key West was a close-knit one and Rafe couldn't for the life of him imagine any of them talking about Emily.

It must have been someone who knew him.

He remembered the way she'd sneaked into his penthouse. Maybe that was where the reporter had picked up the thread of the story. Maybe he'd followed her.

Hell, he had no idea.

He rubbed the back of his neck. He was tired.

"You're not confronting anyone," he said. "I'll go tomorrow and take care of it."

She put her hand on his chest and shoved him back so she could get up from the chair. Standing next to him, she put her hands on her hips and arched one eyebrow at him.

"One—you're not the boss of me. Sorry, I'm just not going to take orders. Two—that rat bastard played me and I want to make sure that doesn't happen again," she said. "So I'll take care of it."

It was late and he was tired of being pulled in too many directions, so perhaps that was why he let his temper slip as he stood up, towering over her. He put his hands on her shoulders and realized all he wanted to do was protect her, and that was the one thing that Emily didn't seem to want from him.

"Dammit, woman. I'm trying to keep you safe. I don't want any of this dirty press to affect you. I need to know that you aren't harmed by it."

"Why?" she asked. "Because you think I can't handle it?"

"Hell, Red. You can handle anything. I am doing this because I care about you and if anything hurt you I wouldn't be able to live with it."

Nine

Rafe pulled her to him and slammed his mouth down on hers, backing her up against the wall. The moment their mouths met his anger died. It felt like too long since he'd held her in his arms. She did that thing with her tongue where she twirled it around his, and he instantly got hard.

He cupped her butt and flexed his fingers, lifting her up until he could rub his erection right over the center of her body. She was naked under her shirt, and he liked the feel of her cool buttocks in his hands. She moved against him and he feathered his finger in a circle around the small of her back. She moaned and arched against him before tunneling her fingers into his hair and holding him to her while she plundered his mouth.

There was too much pent-up emotion between them. They'd been in the same room together three times and each time it hadn't been enough. He wanted her. The way she got to him was unlike anything else he'd ever experienced, and his gut was starting to say he wouldn't find it with anyone else.

He sank to the floor when she sucked his bottom lip between her teeth and bit him lightly. Once he was on the floor, he pushed his hands up her back, felt the way her body arched over his. He rubbed his hand up her delicate spine, finding the sensitive nerves at the back of her neck, tracing a pattern over the skin of her nape.

She pulled back and looked up at him. Her lips were swollen, her face slightly flushed pink, making her freckles more prominent. Her eyes were brilliant in the dim light and he realized he'd never seen anything more beautiful.

He wanted her so much at this moment he couldn't think of anything but getting inside her.

"The other night was a pale imitation of this," she said, her husky voice turning him on.

"Damned straight," he said. He pulled her shirt up over her body and tossed it aside.

He set her back on his thighs as he stretched his legs out and held her there so he could look at her. He took in her breasts, which were slightly larger since her pregnancy, and those darker, fuller nipples. He lightly caressed them, running his finger over first one, then the other. She reached between them and pushed his T-shirt up his body.

He let go of her to rip it off and toss it carelessly to the side. She put her fingers on his pectorals and he flexed them. She sighed and traced her finger around each of his nipples before leaning forward to nip each of them in turn.

He brought his hands back to her breasts, but she took one of them and drew it slowly down the side of her body. He reached around behind her and grabbed her ass, bringing her closer. She rocked her pelvis over the ridge of his erection where it strained against the front of his jeans.

He brought one of his arms up behind her and held her with his hand on the back of her neck as he lowered his head and kissed his way down her neck to her shoulder blade. There was a large strawberry birthmark on her left shoulder and he kissed it, laving it with his tongue before he nibbled his way lower. He dropped small kisses around the full globe of her breast and then moved lower to the underside, biting lightly at the spot where her breast rested against her chest.

She moaned his name and rocked against him as she gripped his sides, trying to bring him closer to her. But he held her where she was. He wasn't ready to let her have free rein over his body. She'd been tormenting him for days with her conversations and the little pieces of her soul that she shared with him almost as if they were an afterthought.

He had her in his arms, but she was hard to hold. So hard to keep. And he was determined that he would keep her.

He sucked at the smooth skin between her breasts and then moved on to her other breast. This one was slightly smaller than its mate. He wanted to know everything about her, to know all these details instead of just being satisfied with sex. He needed more than the physical from her this time. He wanted to lay her completely bare so that maybe he'd have the answers that he'd been seeking.

He brought one of his hands up and slowly drew his finger in circles around her areola. He felt the texture of her nipple changing as it tightened under his finger and then he rubbed his finger back and forth against it until she leaned forward, catching the lobe of his ear between her teeth and biting down hard.

He lifted his head to look into her blue eyes. He swore he could see the same desire in her eyes to get rid of all the questions and doubts that remained between them. But he knew he might just be projecting what he wanted to see. He needed something from her that he couldn't define.

She swiped her tongue around the rim of his ear and he got even harder. Uncomfortable now, he reached between their bodies, distracted by the feel of her wet sex against the back of his fingers. He turned his hand and palmed her. He liked the feel of her springy curls as he rotated his palm against her.

She arched her back and shifted against him. He teased the opening of her body with his finger and then slowly pushed it up into her. She tightened around him. And he felt as if he were going to explode. He wanted to feel her naked flesh against him.

Though he did like her naked on his lap while he was still clothed. He pulled back and looked down at her, wanting to keep this moment in his mind forever.

He used his thumb to find her clit. He tapped it lightly and then made a small circle. She responded instantly. He felt the minute tightening of her body around his finger as he continued to rub his thumb in a circle over her center.

He lowered his mouth to her breast and took her nipple between his lips, swirling his tongue over it and then sucking. Her hands were on his shoulders, nails digging into them as she rocked against his hand. She arched her shoulders and pulled her breast from his mouth.

Their eyes met and all the things he'd been afraid to say seemed to hover in the air around them. He opened his mouth and she leaned forward and kissed him.

She started to rock more quickly. She sucked his tongue deep into her mouth and plunged it back and forth to the same rhythm of his finger inside her body. Her thighs tightened around his hand and he pulled his mouth from hers.

"Come for me," he said, whispering the words against her ear.

Her hips moved more frantically and he added a second finger inside her body as she cried out his name. She thrust her hips rapidly against him and then she shuddered and fell forward, resting her head on his shoulder. Her breath was warm against his neck as she reached her hand down between them and unzipped his jeans.

Her touch through the opening of his pants almost made him come. He felt a drop leak out of him and slowly pulled his hand from her body and got to his feet, lifting her up into his arms. He didn't want this to end too quickly

He carried her down the small hallway and into her bedroom, setting her down on her feet next to the bed. She had wrapped one arm around his shoulder, holding on to him and idly toying with the hair at the back of his neck, while her other arm was awkwardly wedged between them, her hand wrapped around his length.

She stroked him up and down, her finger swirling over the top of him. His hips jerked forward and no matter how much his mind said that he was going to take this slowly, his body had different plans.

He let her body slide down his. She moaned as her hardened nipples rubbed over his chest, and he closed his eyes as he felt the dampness of her core against the front of his boxers.

He stepped back and shoved his pants and underwear down his legs and then nudged her forward until she fell back on the bed. Her legs sprawled apart slightly, her hair fanning out around her head, one brilliant dark red curl falling over her shoulder. She had her hands on the top of her thighs and she watched him with hungry eyes.

He wanted to say something profound because the emotions he felt for her welled up inside him, but instead all he could think about was touching and tasting every inch of her.

"Are you just going to stand there and stare at me?" she asked, a tinge of wry amusement visible on her face.

"I'm debating where to start. Every time we've been together I want to make it last…I haven't had the chance to taste you or to explore every one of those lovely freckles of yours."

"There's plenty of time for that later. I want you now," she said.

Her words lanced through him and his erection jumped. He shook his head. Every time he thought he had the upper hand with Emily she did something to remind him that he was putty in her hands. Now and always.

She reached for his length, circling him with her thumb and forefinger at the root. She slowly drew her hand up, closing the circle of her fingers around him as she did so. Involuntarily he thrust closer to her and she smiled up at him as a drop of precome glistened on the tip of his erection. She swiped her finger over it and then brought it to her mouth.

He groaned and crawled up over her body, and then put his hands on her hips and forced her to move back on the bed. He took her hands in his and drew them up over her head as he settled his hips between hers and the tip of his erection found the moist center of her body.

He drew his hips back and then thrust forward again, entering her slowly. She arched underneath him and yet still he resisted the urge to plunge his way all the way home. She turned her hands under his, laced their fingers together and looked up at him.

"Take me," she said.

He nodded as he drove himself hilt-deep into her body. She sighed and arched against him again and he started to thrust in and out, taking them both closer and closer to the edge. He pulled his hand free of hers and drew it down her side as he rocked back and forth. Going deeper each time and taking them higher and higher.

She ran her finger down his back and he jerked his hips forward as he came. Then he felt her legs tighten around his hips and heard her calling his name as she climaxed.

He kept driving into her until she bit him softly on the shoulder and sighed. She turned her head to face him and he saw the completion on her face. He found her lips with his and gave her a soft, gentle kiss.

Rafe wanted to believe that everything was okay between them but he knew that sex hadn't made it so. From the beginning their bond had been strong and physical. That created its own sort of problems. He wanted to just keep making love to her and pretending that was enough, but he knew it wasn't. And there were things he had to say that she might not want to hear.

But for this moment he wanted to just hold her, look up at the moon and pretend that everything was okay.

Emily woke up in the middle of the night having to go to the bathroom. This was something that had only started in the last week. She had read in one of her prenatal books that things like this were only the beginning.

Rafe was cuddled behind her and propped himself up on an elbow as she climbed from the bed. "You okay?" he asked.

"Yes. Be right back."

He fell back down on the pillow and she knew he was tired. They'd resolved nothing except that they still wanted each other. But she felt as if this time they'd done more than just have sex. Rafe meant more to her than any other guy she'd ever dated, and she acknowledged that it had nothing to do with the fact that he was the father of her child—and yet at the same time had everything to do with that.

He made her feel more alive than anyone else ever had, and that was dangerous. She didn't want to rely on him. He could sleep in her bed and come to her bar. Hell, he could even be involved with their baby, but she didn't want to care for him.

She washed her hands and leaned forward to look at herself in the mirror.

"Don't fall for him," she warned herself. But she sort of already knew that it was too late.

That falling for Rafe was a foregone conclusion now.

He'd come to her in the middle of the night. Wanted to defend her. Everyone knew she could take care of herself, but he still wanted to protect her.

That made her feel so safe. So cherished.

Things that had never mattered to her before tonight.

She shook her head.

He had to want something. There had to be a reason he was here tonight. She wanted it to be for her, but maybe it was about the baby. Now that the world knew about their child, the decisions they'd been making together took on a different quality. Whatever he did could impact his people back in Alma.

She knew that. She wanted it to not matter, but she knew it did.

And she also was very aware that she wasn't cut out to be a queen or consort or whatever the hell they had in Alma.

Maybe that was why he was here.

She left the bathroom and stood in the doorway leading back into the bedroom, watching him as he lay sleeping, his big, strong, sexy body taking up too much of her bed, his face relaxed in sleep. He didn't seem as if he had an agenda. He didn't act as if there were some reason he was in her bed other than that he wanted to be there.

But she knew there had to be more.

She lived in the real world, and stained glass mermaid aside, Rafe had always been very real with her. . When they'd spent their one weekend together, he'd made it clear that would be it. As had she. And when she'd barged in on him in Miami and told him she was pregnant he hadn't pretended they were suddenly a couple.

"I thought you got lost, Red."

She thought she did, too. The first time she'd looked into his hazel eyes.

"I almost did. Why are you here, Rafe?" she asked.

"Come back to bed," he said.

She walked over and sat on the edge of the bed, but he lifted the sheets and gestured for her to come closer. She wanted to. She started to lie down in the curve of his body but stopped herself.

"I need some answers. So far all we've done is establish what we both already knew. We want each other. We have some kind of lust that won't be denied. But I need some answers."

"Okay."

"Okay?"

"Sure. Ask your questions," he said, sitting up and propping his back on the headboard. "I figured we'd do this in the morning."

"I don't think I can sleep until I know if you are going to take my child from me."

She hadn't meant to say it that way. But it was 3:00 a.m. and her guard was down. Her fears were all around her. Rafe was a powerful man before she even factored in the fact that he was about to become the ruler of a foreign land.

"Hell. No. I'm not going to take our child from you," he said. "Why would you think I'd do that? I'm not an asshole."

She swallowed hard. "I know you aren't. But we both know I'm not the kind of woman your family has been hoping you'll marry. And now that the world knows I'm carrying the king of Alma's child, I think the stakes have changed."

He reached for her. Took her hand in his and brought it to his mouth. He dropped a warm kiss in the center of her palm before placing her hand on his chest right over his heart.

"I haven't changed, Red. I'm still the man you know. I'm not going to let anything change me."

She wanted to believe him. But the monarchy was bigger than Rafe, whether he wanted to admit it or not.

He tugged her off balance and into his arms. Rolling until she was tucked underneath him. He kissed her long and slow, and she felt her fears for the future disappearing slowly.

In his embrace she felt as if things would work out, but she feared that was false hope until she knew how he felt about her. Until she had some promises… But she'd never had a man make her promises. Never wanted them until now. Until Rafe. She needed something from him, but she was afraid to admit that even to herself.

How the hell was she going to tell him that she wanted him to be by her side? Not because of the baby, but because she needed him.

She tipped her head, closing her eyes and pretending that she had the answers she needed. But she knew that things were even more complicated now than they had been before.

Ten

Rafe woke with the sun, since he was still on European time, and left Emily sleeping quietly in her bed. Last night he'd almost lost her. He still wasn't sure he'd said the right thing or even done enough to keep her. But today he intended to change all of that.

He went out to his car and retrieved the bag that Jose had packed and brought it into the house. He scanned the street while he did so, but saw no reporters hanging around, which was reassuring. As were the two cop cars parked at each end of her street. There was no foot traffic on her block today either.

He found eggs and the fixings for an omelet in Emily's fridge and set to making breakfast for her. His hands were sweating when he put it all on the breakfast tray he'd found in her pantry. He dashed outside to pick a hibiscus from the flowering bush in her backyard and put it in a small teacup with some water. Then he patted his pocket to make sure the ring hadn't disappeared and walked back to her bedroom.

With any other woman this kind of gesture might be enough to make her swoon. But Rafe suspected it might not be enough with Red.

She was still asleep on her side with his pillow tucked up against her. She looked small and vulnerable as she slept. During the day she was a virago, constantly moving and challenging everything in her path. But like this it was easy to see she wasn't as invincible as she wanted the world to believe. Feeling like a voyeur, he put the tray on her dresser and snapped a quick photo of her with his iPhone.

Then he walked over to the bed and sat down

next to her. He was tempted to slide back under the sheets with her. Make love to her again, but sex was tearing away layers that he usually used to insulate himself against women. And he couldn't afford to let Emily any closer to him than she already was.

Love was a fairy tale, one he wasn't too sure existed. He'd seen what his father had done for love and how that had torn their entire family apart.

"Em…"

"Um…"

"Wake up, sleepyhead."

She blinked up at him and shoved her hand through her thick red hair, pushing it back off her face. She sat up, ran her tongue over her teeth and then looked at him. "Aren't you chipper in the morning."

He was. He'd always been a morning person, but he sensed that she wasn't and decided silence was the better part of valor. "I'm still on a different time zone. I brought you coffee."

"I can only have decaf," she said.

"That's what I made since it was on the counter next to your machine," he said.

"Thank you," she said, reaching for the mug. Blowing on the surface of the hot liquid before taking a sip, she closed her eyes, seeming to savor it as that first swallow went down.

He felt himself stir and shook his head.

Really. Was there nothing she could do that wouldn't turn him on?

"You haven't tried the omelet yet," he said as he knelt on the bed and settled the tray over her lap.

"No. For trying to protect me. For doing this," she said. "I'm just not the kind of woman men usually do this kind of thing for."

"Yes, you are," he said.

She wrinkled her brow as she stared over at him. He took off the lid that he'd used to cover her plate so it wouldn't get cold and smiled over at her.

"Are you arguing with me?"

"Yeah, I am. I made you breakfast in bed, so

clearly you are the right type. The other guys in your life haven't measured up."

She put her coffee on the tray and leaned over to kiss him. It was a little clumsy and tasted of sleepy woman and coffee. He wanted more but she pulled back.

"You're saying all the right things this morning."

"I try. How's your stomach?" he asked. "I didn't even think about your morning sickness."

"I'm not sure I can eat too much, but the coffee seems okay right now."

"That's good. I had Jose get me a bunch of books on pregnancy but haven't had a chance to read them yet," he said.

He wanted to know what was going to be happening to her so he could anticipate her needs. Make everything easier for her.

They shared the breakfast he made and then he set the tray to the side and lay next to her on the bed. "Do you have to work today?"

"No. Do you?"

"No. I'm supposed to lie low," he said. And

make everything with Emily right in the eyes of the world. But that part was still better left unspoken for now.

"Good. What do you want to do?"

"Well…"

He pulled her into his arms and then rolled over, bracing his body on top of hers. He put his hand on her stomach and dropped a quick kiss there before looking up at her. He worked his free hand into the pocket of his pants and pulled out the ring box.

"I'm hoping that you'll agree to marry me, Red."

He put the ring box on her stomach and then opened it up so she could see the thin band with the pear-shaped diamond. He'd chosen the band lined with aquamarine because that stone reminded him of her eyes. He shifted to his side, knelt next to her and stared down into her heart-shaped face. "I hope you'll say yes."

She stared up at him for a long moment and he had the feeling she wasn't going to say yes. What had he done wrong? He'd made the big romantic gesture; he'd purchased a ring that reminded him of her.

He was being a good guy. Doing everything by the book of romance. He'd seen his sister reading fairy tales and *Cosmo* so he knew that he had to come across as modern and thoughtful but also deliver on all Emily's secret dreams.

It was a big ask of a man who was used to women falling for him. Especially after the time he'd spent on Alma with Dita and her ilk fawning over him.

"What did I do wrong?"

"Nothing," she said. "I like the ring and the breakfast, but I like my mermaid, too."

He processed that.

The mermaid had been a stroke of genius. Well, really it had been the gesture of a man who missed his woman.

"Doesn't matter if you wear the ring, you're mine."

"I'm yours?"

"We both know it. There isn't a wannabe debutante in all the world who can compare to you, Red."

She gave him a haughty look and then ruined it by laughing. "I know it."

"What about you?"

"Huh?"

"Is there anyone else in your life?"

"Would I be with you if there was?" she asked. "I like you way more than I should, Rafael. Your life is literally worlds away from here but I can't help letting you into my house and my bed. I'm just trying to keep us both from making a mistake."

Maybe he could convince her to say yes. This was the opening he needed. "It's not a mistake. Trust me. Together, we can take on anything."

"For now. But what happens when the newness of being lovers wears off and we have a baby who doesn't sleep through the night? And you have to run a kingdom?"

He saw where she was coming from. And realized the fears she had stemmed from the fact that she didn't know him. Didn't realize how unstoppable he was once he made his mind up.

"I said I'd give you time to get to know me, and once you do, you will know that isn't going to be an issue," he said.

Frankly this shocked her. Rafe didn't strike her as all that traditional. And she knew that he was still trying to figure out the next few months of his life. She wasn't going to be his lifesaver. His safety valve. And that's what this felt like.

"No." The little girl who never had a mom and a dad desperately wanted her to say yes. But she'd learned long ago that the things she wanted most were the ones that made her make the dumbest decisions. And marriage wasn't something to be entered into lightly. Rafe was going to be king. He should have a wife who was in it for the long haul.

He was going to have to do a lot of work to make the monarchy stick in Alma. *Alma.* She wasn't even sure where it was. Maybe she should have looked that up on the internet instead of ogling pictures of Rafe as he toured the island nation. But she hadn't.

"No?" he asked. "Red, think this through."

"I can't marry you," she said. She could, but it wasn't under these circumstances. If he'd asked her the first time she'd shown up on his doorstep pregnant she might have said yes. But too much had happened since then and she couldn't trust his motives.

They knew each other so much better now than they had a mere two weeks earlier, but still not well enough. Or from her perspective, maybe too well. She wanted that man who sent her the stained glass to fall down on his knees and beg her to marry him.

That wasn't going to happen. Rafe liked her. He wanted her but he didn't love her.

"Are you asking me because I'm pregnant?" she asked at last.

He rolled off the bed and got to his feet. He put his hands on his lean hips and stood there as if he could will her to change her mind. She wished he'd put a shirt on, because his bare chest was a tempting distraction.

But not enough of one that she'd say yes to this. She knew if she said yes she'd want him to love her. Why? She'd been fine with lust until this moment, and now she wanted professions of deep emotion from him. Emotion she wasn't prepared to admit she felt for him.

They didn't love each other. She had never thought she was one of those women who needed it, but in her heart she knew she did. She wasn't as practical as she'd expected to be when it came to Rafe. He was arguing that they'd be stronger together, and she thought if they loved each other then he might be right. But a couple who married for the sake of a child? That seemed like a steep hill to climb.

Maybe it was because her mother had never compromised and married that Emily felt so strongly about this. But she couldn't help it. She wasn't going to marry him for any reason. Unless he fell in love with her and proved it in some way that would convince her. She liked him. She cared about him and she had no intention of isolating him from his child. But marriage?

No. Definitely not.

"Partly. I'm traditional, Red. You know that. I want our baby to have my name. And to know who I am. We can do that so much better together," he said. He scrubbed one hand over his eyes and then sat down on the edge of the bed with his back toward her. "Every child needs a mom and a dad. Didn't you miss having a dad?"

"I did," she said. "But I found my way without one. And Harry's sort of filled the role for me. It's all I needed."

"I don't want our kid to have a relationship with some future boyfriend of yours," he said.

"Don't. Don't think of any of that. We are going to get to know each other. We will figure this out."

She crawled over to him and wrapped her arms around his shoulders, leaning her head on his chest to look at him. "Marriage like this isn't a solution. We'd have to be more businesslike and we aren't. The way you get to me…it's all I can do to remind myself every day that you belong on the throne of Alma and I have no place by your side."

He covered her hands with his and clasped them to his chest. "You might."

She shook her head and slid around on the bed next to him. He was so serious, this man of hers. "Is that why you are asking me?"

"Yes. I care for you, Emily," he said. "I want what's best for you and our child. And if you are my fiancée I can protect you from the media. I can bring the full force of the Montoro name and reputation to bear against these people. I can do it now, but they will just glom onto the fact that I'm not marrying you or taking you to Alma. Being my fiancée will make everything easier."

She felt the sincerity in his words. Understood that he was willing to tie his life to hers to keep her safe. But for how long? Because she knew that she didn't want to leave Key West, and there was no way he could rule from here.

"I can't."

"Don't say no. Think about it. Let's see if I can change your mind," he said.

She had no doubt that he could. If she spent time with him and fell any deeper for him then she'd say yes. She'd exchange her life for his. And she knew herself well enough to know that she'd be angry with that.

"How?"

"Let's date and get to know each other. In a few weeks I'll ask you again," he said.

"How will we do that? Do I have to fly to Alma?"

"No. I'm in Miami to wrap up a few business deals. So while I'm here let's date."

"Okay. But what if the answer is still no. What then?" she asked.

"I'm pretty determined it won't be," he said. "And I've never lost a challenge."

"Never?"

"Nope. I'm not afraid to do whatever I have to in order to win you over."

She believed him but she also knew this

decision wasn't his alone. "What about your family?"

"Leave them to me. I'd like you to come to Miami Beach next week, stay at my place and meet everyone who's here with me at a dinner. Would you do that?"

She pursed her lips but then nodded. "What day? I'll have to check my schedule at the bar."

"I was hoping for Friday night. But I know that's one of your busiest nights and this relationship isn't all about me. So you tell me which day works for you," he said.

She reached for her phone on the nightstand and checked her work schedule. Harry was going to transition her to the daytime shift starting next week since her pregnancy had really started showing.

She texted Beau, the other bartender, to see if he'd fill in for her on Friday and Saturday. He was always looking for more money and immediately responded that he could.

"Friday is fine," she said.

"Great. Now what should we do today?" he asked.

"I have a few ideas," she said. "But you're going to need swim trunks."

"I packed for a couple of days. I'm good."

The beach that Emily took him to later that afternoon was deserted and well off the beaten path. They had to carry the paddleboard from her car through a stand of mangroves to the water's edge. There were cicadas chirping and the smell of salt water mixed with ripe vegetation. It was so Florida.

The heat beat down on his back and he wore a baseball cap and large sunglasses to protect his face from the sun. Emily had surprised him by giving him a lecture about the dangers of skin cancer even to someone with his olive complexion. So he'd donned her SPF 50 sun cream and the hat even though he never burned.

Her mothering had charmed him. And it was mothering. She'd kind of ensured he had the cream on and taken her time rubbing it on his back, which had led them back to the bedroom. Hence the late start at the beach.

She'd also packed a cooler of fruit juice, sandwiches and veggies. He'd seldom—okay, never—taken a day like this. It was a Monday. He should be in Miami getting ready for the weekly management meeting where he should be discussing the new shipping deal and getting all the routes worked out for their customers, but truth be told he wouldn't trade this for anything.

The way his family had reacted when they'd landed had worried Rafe. He had the sinking feeling in his gut that they were going to make him choose between Emily and their baby and the throne. And as usual when he got his back up that meant he got stubborn. He wasn't too sure he wanted the throne, but he wasn't about to let his family force him out of it.

He had the Coleman cooler in one hand and the paddleboard under his other arm. She'd said she could help carry stuff but he'd said no. He found that he liked making gallant gestures.

This morning when she'd turned down his proposal, he'd realized she hadn't had a lot of men doing that for her. And he was determined to convince her that he was the right guy for her.

On that front, he wasn't backing down.

"This spot looks good. We can leave the cooler here. Actually," she said with a blush, "we could have left it in the car. It's not that far to walk back for a snack."

"Then why did I carry it down here?"

She crossed her arms over her chest and gave him a chagrined look. "Because you were so stubborn about me helping carry the board. I hate being bossed."

"You mentioned that. But this isn't bossing, it's pampering. Like when you insisted I wear sunscreen."

She started to argue but then stuck her tongue out at him. "You're right. But don't make a habit of it."

He threw his head back and laughed. She kept him on his toes no matter how much he didn't want to admit it. He liked the challenge of being with her.

"So you've never been on a paddleboard before?" she asked.

"Nope. Never even surfed. I am scuba certified though. Want to do that instead?"

"Yes but the water around here isn't that deep. Snorkeling would be better. We could do that tonight. I know a gorgeous place where we can go at sunset. In fact, if my mom doesn't mind, we can take her boat," she said.

"I'd like to meet your mom," he said.

She got really still. "Why?"

"Because she's your mom," Rafe said. "Why else?"

"Don't try to get her on your side with this engagement thing, okay?"

He put the board on the sand and walked over to her, putting his finger under her chin and tipping her head back so he could see her eyes under the bill of her baseball cap. "When you say yes—and I'm betting you eventually do—it will be because you've decided you want to marry me. Not because I pressured you into saying yes. Got it?"

She punched him playfully in the shoulder and ran down toward the waterline. "I've got it. Get that board and come on, Your Majesty. It's time for your first lesson."

Rafe followed her to the water and they spent the next thirty minutes with her showing him how to get his balance on the board. Finally Emily decided he could take a turn rowing and he got about two strokes in before he fell into the warm Atlantic Ocean.

He glanced at the shore to find her standing there laughing.

"I bet it wasn't easy for you at first," he said as he swam back to shore with the board.

"I don't remember. I've been on the water since before I could walk," she said.

"So you grew up here?"

"Since I was three, so I think that counts, doesn't it?"

"Pretty much. I was born in Coral Gables and grew up there," he said.

"Florida native."

"Well, just my generation," he said.

He looked at her and the future suddenly didn't seem as nebulous as it always had. The future was real and it was staring back at him with red hair and blue eyes. And that made Alma seem farther away than ever.

"Why don't you stand on the end of my board and look studly and I'll take you on a tour of this inlet?" she asked.

"Studly?"

"Yeah. Oh, is that an insult to your masculinity?" she teased. "I figured after that dunking you gave yourself you might like to play it safe."

He rushed her, scooping her up in his arms and carrying her into the water. "I never play it safe, Red. And I'm not the only one who's going to get a dunking."

He fell backward into the water, keeping her in his arms and drenching them both. She swiveled in his arms and when they both surfaced she kissed him. One kiss led to another and

Rafe realized he was having the best afternoon of his life.

He told himself it was just the relief at being away from the pressures of leading Alma and Montoro Enterprises, but his heart said his future was tied to this woman.

Eleven

Emily had felt more at ease staring down a belligerent drunk at Shady Harry's than she did standing in the formal dining room of the Montoros' Coral Gables mansion holding a tonic water with lime in one hand. Rafael III had turned his back on her when she entered the room with Rafe, who had been called away by Jose. He'd seemed reluctant to leave her but she'd urged him to go. She was rethinking that opinion now.

Juan Carlos looked less than pleased to actually meet her and the PR guy Geoff had muttered under his breath that she was no style icon. Well, who was? She was a real person. She wasn't going to apologize for who she was.

Tia Isabella had been feeling well enough to be up with the family. She and her nurse were in one corner with Rafe's sister Bella. Tia Isabella was in a wheelchair and her hands and head kept shaking because of her advanced Parkinson's. When her nurse invited Emily over to join the women, she was grateful. Isabella had beautiful white hair and was the only one to smile at Emily and make her feel truly welcome.

"Hello, Emily," Bella said, coming up behind her and putting her arm around her.

"Bella right? Or should I call you Lady Bella?"

"Just Bella is fine. You look like you are about to bolt."

"I am."

"Well, don't. I've never seen Rafe like this before."

"Like what?"

"Unsettled."

"That's good. He's too sure he knows it all," Emily said.

Bella laughed and Emily noticed that her brothers smiled at the sound. "Rafe mentioned going out on your mother's boat…Is it a yacht?"

Emily realized that Bella was really in a different world. "No. She's a marine biologist. Her boat is like the station wagon of the sea."

"Did you grow up on it? Like Jacques Cousteau's family?"

"No. She had a grant that enabled her to return to Key West every night," Emily said.

"Sounds fascinating."

They were called to dinner and Rafe rejoined her. "How'd it go?"

"Most of your family hate me. If they could make me disappear they would," she said.

"They don't hate you," Rafe said.

"Don't lie to me," she retorted.

"Well, it's not you. It's the fact that I am putting our family's return to Alma and the throne in a very delicate state. No one, not even me, wants that."

Emily wanted to apologize but she couldn't. She wasn't sorry she was having his baby or that she'd gotten to know him. But she was sorry that they'd met now when his life wasn't his own. And when his family would never approve of her.

The next two weeks were busy and though Rafe would be happy to stop flying back and forth between Key West and Miami, he enjoyed every second he spent with Emily.

Tonight he was cruising toward the setting sun with Jessica, Harry and Emily. His first meeting with Emily's mom had been tense but ever since Emily had wrapped her arm around his waist and given her mom a stubborn look, Jessica had been sort of friendly toward him. Harry on the other hand looked as if he was going to need more than a stern look from Emily.

If he didn't know that they were going night diving, he'd have been worried.

"Beer?" Harry asked, walking up to him

where he sat on a padded bench at the stern of the boat.

"Nah, I'm good."

Harry sat down next to him and took a sip of his Corona. Emily and her mom were at the helm of the boat talking and laughing as they got out of the no-wake zone. Suddenly Jessica hit the throttle and they were flying full speed across the ocean.

As the wind buffeted Rafe, Harry leaned forward, shouting a little to be heard over the noise. "What are your plans with our girl?"

"None of your business," Rafe shouted back. "No disrespect but you and I both know she'll skin us alive if we discuss it behind her back."

Harry threw his head back and gave a great shout of laughter. The other man was big and solid, but no taller than Rafe. And he'd noticed over the past couple weeks how Harry watched out for Emily as no other adult in her life had.

Her mom, though sweet and loving toward Emily, spent most of her time thinking about her research and reapplying for grants. Her entire world was the ocean and the creatures in it.

It had been startling to realize that in essence Emily had raised herself. That was probably why she was so tough, so feisty and so damned independent. She had a lifetime of doing things on her own. How the hell was he going to convince her that she needed him by her side?

But he understood why the arguments he'd been making hadn't worked. What was it that she needed? The one thing she couldn't give herself, he suspected, was the key to bringing her around.

His phone buzzed. He'd hoped they'd be out of range but no such luck. He looked down and saw he had received a text from Geoff Standings once again asking again if he could run with their release announcing Rafe's engagement to Emily.

He texted back no and then shut his phone off. His family didn't get how delicate the situation was and thought that he could order her to marry him.

As if.

"Just know if you hurt her, bud, I'm coming after you," Harry said with that slightly maniacal grin of his.

"That's the last thing I want to do," Rafe said loudly.

Jessica killed the engines and his words sort of echoed around the boat as everything went quiet.

"What's the last thing you want to do?" Emily said, coming over and sitting on his lap. She wrapped her arm around his shoulders and reached over to take Harry's beer. "No drinking and diving, Harry. That's dangerous."

"It was one beer, kiddo. And barely that," Harry said, getting up and going over to Jessica.

"What is the last thing you'd do?" she asked Rafe when they were alone. He heard the sounds of Jessica and Harry getting the scuba gear ready behind them.

"Hurt you," he said, looking down into her pretty blue eyes.

"No promises, remember?" she said, standing up.

He grabbed her wrist, keeping her by his side as he had a sudden flash of insight into what it was she needed but was afraid to ask for. She needed promises and she needed them to be kept.

"I'm making this one, Red. And I'm keeping it," he said.

"What about Alma and your family?" she asked.

"What about them? That has nothing to do with you and me."

She snorted and shook her head. "It has everything to do with us. I'm complicating things. I think we both know that dinner with your family didn't go very well because of it. They think…heck, I have no idea what they think. But they don't like me much."

He wondered if that were true. He believed his family didn't feel one way or another about Emily. It was him they were frustrated with. They needed him to make her his fiancée or get her out of the picture. They needed him to clean up his act so they could continue with the coronation plans. But he wasn't playing their game.

"It's me they're pissed at," he said. "I'm sure they will like you once they get to know you."

She gave him an incredulous look. "I thought you were going to be a king of Alma, not fairy-tale land."

He laughed. "I am."

"You two done flirting?" Harry called, interrupting their argument. "Ready to do some diving?"

"Yes, we are, Harry," Emily said, walking over and getting her gear on.

Rafe followed her, wishing things were as simple as flirting. But nothing with her ever was.

He joined her family and went over the side of the boat after they'd put the diver down flag in the water. He noticed that everyone scattered in their own direction.

He followed close by Emily's side and reached for her hand, linking them together. She looked at him for a moment, her face not very clear behind the glass of her scuba mask, and then led him through the underwater world. She pointed out different species of fish and coral, and caught up in the natural beauty of his surroundings, he forgot his troubles. There was something very peaceful about snorkeling. But when they surfaced, he knew that nothing had changed in their world.

But he felt strongly that he and Emily had crossed a bridge into new territory.

"That was nice," she said, treading water next to him.

"Yes, it was. Exactly what I need after a day full of meetings and demands," he said as they took off their tanks and put them in the boat.

"What is?"

Time with the woman he loved.

Shock held him in place as he realized that he did love her.

Versailles was the most famous Cuban restaurant in Miami. Hell, probably the world. Rafe had a night away from his family planned for himself and Emily. And grabbing Cuban sandwiches at his favorite restaurant was exactly the right sort of tone he wanted to set.

He needed Emily to accept his proposal, but pressuring her wasn't the way to get the job done. So he'd been as smooth as he could be, trying not to pressure her into making a decision that he needed from her. And the sooner, the better.

Every day she waited just made his family more anxious. At first it was just the inner circle of his father, brother and cousin, but now his more distant relatives—even his ill Tia Isabella—were asking him when he was going to announce his engagement.

He suspected Tia Isabella was being egged on by his cousin Juan Carlos, the one who wanted the family's return to the throne of Alma to be…triumphant. Not mired in scandal.

Rafe got that.

He'd even had a meeting with Montoro Enterprises' board of directors today. They had been pretty threatening; the upshot was, if he screwed up things in Alma he might not be CEO for much longer.

But the more his family pushed, the less he responded. None of that mattered tonight. The dinner with Emily hadn't gone well. And they'd called a "family" meeting to discuss the matter tomorrow.

Tonight he was going to seduce the hell out of Emily and secure her as his fiancée and then go into the meeting with his family he had scheduled for tomorrow and take control of the situation.

Waiting on Emily, waiting on his family— he felt shackled on all sides. He couldn't take action the way he needed to so that he could move forward.

He and Emily were seated against the wall in the glass-and-mirrored main room of the restaurant. All around him he heard people talking in Spanish. The Cuban dialect was different from the Castilian Spanish that many of the people of Alma used. Cuban Spanish was much more familiar to him.

"So what's on the agenda tonight?" Emily said after they had placed their order.

"Dinner, dancing and then I'll show you the harbor from my rooftop patio. I think you will be impressed."

"I'm never not impressed by you, Rafe."

"Thank you. Perhaps I should ask you that question again?"

She shook her head and her face got a little pinched. "Please don't. Can we have tonight and just be Emily and Rafe, not the future king and his errant pregnant lover?"

He realized that she was facing a different kind of pressure. She'd agreed to come to Miami for a few days after a group of paparazzi had staked out Shady Harry's in Key West. It was either take the security offered by staying in his penthouse or go out on the boat with her mother.

He was pleased she'd chosen to come to him. He felt as if they had gotten so much closer over the last few weeks together.

"Yes, we can," he said.

"Great. So tell me why you picked this restaurant. I know it's famous and all that, but I wouldn't expect you to be a regular here."

He leaned back in the chair. "Well, the food is the best. You can't find a better Cuban sandwich anywhere in the city. But when I was younger, about ten or so, our mom used to bring Gabe, Bella and me here for dinners on the nights when our dad was in one of his moods and ranting all over the place. And later it was the first place she took us when we got Gabe back."

"Where'd he go?" Emily asked.

"In his early twenties, he was kidnapped while working for our South American division. He ultimately escaped. When we got him back, Mom packed us all up and brought us here. I always associate this place with happy times."

"Where is your mom?" she asked.

"She's remarried and pretty much enjoying her life now that she's out from under the burden of her marriage to our father."

"Do you see her at all?"

"I don't see her very often. But we text. It's enough for me," he said.

She nodded. "It's like that with my mom. I know other people have these crazy-close relationships with their parents but that was never us. She raised me to think for myself and do things for myself."

"Same," Rafe said. "My father gave me the legacy…that sort of feeling of pride in being a Montoro, and my mom gave me the strength to stand on my own while I carry out my version of what that means."

Emily reached across the table and linked their hands together. "I wonder what we will give our baby?"

"Probably everything we never had and always wanted," Rafe said.

Their food arrived and their conversation drifted to lighter topics like bands and books and movies. Everything but the one thing Rafe wanted to discuss. But she'd asked for time, for an evening where they were like every other young couple out on a date.

And he struggled to give it to her. This felt like a game she was playing, and if he wasn't so sure of her confusion about what to do with him, he'd demand an answer. But he knew she wasn't acting maliciously. She was pregnant by a man she hadn't intended to get to know better. The fact that they liked each other as much as they did was fate.

Fate.

Was that what this was?

They weren't like everyone else. They never were going to be. And the fact that Emily wanted them to be didn't make him feel confident for their future together. It started a niggling bit of doubt in the seat of his soul where he'd been confident until now that he could have it all. The throne, his child and Emily by his side.

The rhythm of Little Havana pulsed around them as they walked up Calle Ocho. Rafe reached out and grabbed her hand, lacing their fingers together. Tonight they were pretending that nothing else existed.

But she was aware of the reporters who had followed them from Rafe's South Beach penthouse and were now probably taking photos of them. She wore a Carolina Herrera dress she'd found in a vintage shop earlier in the week. It was a cocktail number in turquoise that hugged her curves on top and had a plunging neckline that gave way to a full skirt that masked her small baby bump.

Everything had been different between her and Rafe since earlier in the week when he'd come diving with her in Key West.

She couldn't put her finger on it, but she knew a lot of it had to do with the new feelings she had for him. It was silly to call it anything but love. Except that she wasn't too sure what love was.

Her mom and she had a relationship based on mutual respect and caring. She could count on one hand the times her mom had told her she loved her. It wasn't that Emily felt unlovable before this; it was just that she struggled to believe these feelings were real.

"Have you been here before?" he asked as they approached the club.

"Little Havana?" she asked.

He nodded.

"Yes. This club—no. I'm not usually on the celebrity radar…though in this dress, I bet I could get in without you tonight."

"You might be able to," Rafe agreed. "The owner and I went to school together."

"The hottie baseball player?"

"He's married. And you're spoken for," Rafe said.

"Am I?"

"You are. We could make it official. I've been carrying your ring around in my pocket."

"Not tonight," she said. She was closer to saying yes. The more time they spent together, the more she realized that being his wife was…well, exactly what she wanted.

"Prepare to be amazed," he said. "They pulled out all the stops with this club."

Emily's breath caught as they were waved past the line of waiting guests and through the grand entrance. The Chihuly chandelier in the lobby was exquisite. But then when wasn't a Chihuly glamorous?

The club was divided into several different areas. The main floor in front of the stage was a huge dance area surrounded by high-stooled tables and cozy booths set in darkened alcoves. On the second floor, where they were headed tonight, was a mezzanine that overlooked the main club and featured a Latin-inspired dance floor. The hottest Latin groups performed there. Regular people and celebrities mingled, brought together by the sexy samba beats of the music.

"Rafael! Hey, dude," said a tall, broad-shouldered man coming over to them. "Do I have to genuflect now?"

Rafe grabbed the man's hand and did that guy hug that was part shoulder bump, part slap on the back before they stepped apart. "Only you do."

The other man shook his head. "I'm going to

pass on that. Why don't you introduce me to your lovely lady?"

"Emily Fielding," Rafe said. "Eric Rubio. He owns this place."

Emily held her hand out to Eric, who took it in his, winked at Rafe and then kissed it. Emily laughed at the easy camaraderie between the two men. As they made their way upstairs to the dance club, she realized that this was the first time she'd seen Rafe so relaxed in Miami.

Emily suspected it was because he was away from the Montoros and the decisions they wanted from him. She knew that she felt the pressure, and it wasn't even directed at her.

She should just say yes to his proposal. She wanted to make everything easier for him, and her taking her time and trying to figure out what she felt for him and if he would always be there when she needed him to be was just making everything harder for Rafe.

Eric left them as the music started, and Rafe held his hand out to her and led her to the dance floor.

They spent the night dancing to salsa music, their bodies brushing against each other, fanning the flames of the desire that was always there between them.

She wished for a moment they could go back to the people they'd been when they'd first met. Just two lusty twentysomethings instead of a man and woman who knew too much about each other.

"You okay?" Rafe asked.

She nodded, but as she looked into those hazel eyes of his she realized she'd probably never be just okay again. All the debating in her mind about whether she loved him or not had been another diversion.

She went up on tiptoe and kissed him, pouring the emotions that she was too scared to admit to into that embrace. His hands skimmed down her sides to her hips and he held her pressed close to him. It felt as if everything dropped away but the two of them.

"Let's get out of here," Rafe said, taking her hand and leading her out the door.

Twelve

Emily wasn't having a good morning. When Rafe's alarm went off, she sprang out of bed and ran to his bathroom to throw up. The morning sickness, which had been waning, was back with a vengeance today. But then she was still in the first trimester. It had seemed as if months had passed, but in reality it was only four weeks since she'd confronted Rafe here in his penthouse. Ten weeks since she'd gotten pregnant.

Yet her entire world had changed.

She suspected it was partially nerves, since Rafe had a big meeting with his family this morning. One that she wasn't invited to attend. He hadn't said much but it had put a damper on their evening once they'd gotten home and he'd finally read all the texts from his cousin and brother reminding him about the meeting. She thought of her little family and how her mom was never one to pressure her into making a decision. But knew she was comparing apples and oranges. Rafe was in line to become king of Alma. There was nothing in Fielding family history that even came close to that.

Both of them knew that this time of dating and getting to know each other was over. She'd overheard a very tense conversation between Rafe and his cousin Juan Carlos last night that didn't sound too promising. She rinsed her mouth out and splashed some water on her face, looking up in the mirror to see Rafe standing there. Simply watching her.

"You okay?" he asked, a gentle smile on his face. He wore only a pair of boxer briefs and she was struck again by how handsome he was. How much she loved every inch of his strong muscled body. "I didn't know what to do. I hate that you get sick in the mornings."

"Yes," she said, taking a hand towel and drying her face. "How are you?"

"I'm fine," he said. "Will you accompany me to the office? We can take the helicopter back to Key West after my meetings are over."

She nodded. "Sounds great."

"I need to shower and shave," he said.

There was an awkwardness between them this morning that hadn't been there in a long time. She wondered if he'd changed his mind about marrying her. Wondered if he wished that he'd just paid her off when she'd come here to tell him that she was pregnant. She just hoped that he didn't regret coming to Key West and Shady Harry's bar and spending that first weekend with her. But the man she'd come to know was now hidden away behind his official Montoro facade.

She knew his attitude had everything to do with his family. He seemed angry and a little bit hurt. And she was scared. For the first time she faced the very real possibility that she might be losing him.

She thought it telling that he hadn't asked her again to marry him this morning. She assumed the time for that had passed. Maybe he wasn't in the mood to pacify his family anymore.

He turned the large shower on and she watched him get into it. For a long minute she stood there before the pain she felt radiating from him made her move.

She undressed and got into the shower cubicle with him. He was facing the wall with his face turned upward to the spray and she just wrapped her arms around him and put her face between his shoulder blades.

She held him to her, trying to give him her strength and that love she hadn't found the words to express yet. Even in her own heart and head.

He turned around, put his hands on her waist and brought his mouth down on hers. She felt the desperation in the embrace, the feeling that after this moment everything would change. He caressed her back, his palms settling on her butt as he pulled her closer to him, anchoring her body and his together.

She kissed him back, wrapped her legs around his hips and trusted that he'd hold her. And he did. He took a step forward and she felt the cold marble wall at her back. Then Rafe adjusted his hips and thrust up into her.

He filled her completely and just stayed still for a moment while her body adjusted to having him inside her. She ran her hands up and down his back, pushing her tongue deep into his mouth. She needed more and the way he was rocking into her sent sparks of sensation up her body.

He palmed her breasts and broke the kiss, lowering his head to take one of her nipples in his mouth. His strong sucking made everything inside her clench. She felt the first waves of her orgasm roll through her.

She grabbed his shoulders and arched her back to try to take him deeper and he started thrusting harder and faster into her. His mouth found hers again; he tangled his hand in her hair and pulled her head back as he thrust deeper into her.

She dug her nails into his shoulders, felt her body driving toward climax again and moaned deep in her throat as a second, deeper orgasm rolled through her. Rafe ripped his mouth from hers and made a feral sound as he thrust his hips forward and came inside her.

He turned and leaned against the wall. She rested her head on his shoulder as her pulse slowly returned to normal. She let her legs slide down his and stood there in his arms. He didn't let her go. Just kept stroking her back and not saying a word.

She realized she was crying and really didn't understand why. Maybe it was because she had the answer to the question about her love for him. It was true and deep. And she understood that now because she was willing to walk away from him if that was what it took for him to have all he wanted.

Jose was waiting in Rafe's office when they got to the headquarters of Montoro Enterprises.

His trusty assistant had a cup of decaf coffee waiting for Emily and a Red Bull for Rafe. He also had a file that needed Rafe's attention before he went into the meeting.

"Jose, I've heard there is a sculpture garden in the building," Emily said, as Rafe skimmed his papers. She was dressed in a scoop-neck blouse, a pair of white denim capris and two-inch platform sandals. She'd left her hair down to curl over her shoulders.

Rafe thought she looked beautiful, but there was a hint of vulnerability to her. One that had been there since she'd dashed to the bathroom from their bed this morning. Nothing he'd done had taken it away. And that was a horrible feeling for a man to know he wasn't able to protect his woman.

"There is the Montoro collection and exhibit. It's on the third floor. Would you like me to show you to it?" Jose asked.

"If Rafe doesn't need you," she said.

"I'm good," Rafe said. Emily gave him a little wave and then walked out of the room with Jose.

The papers that Jose had given him to review showed him the main points of the new constitution of Alma. And he noticed that the part Jose had highlighted dealt with royal marriage. Since they were just reestablishing the monarchy, the rules were strict. Of course, existing marriages would be honored. In cases of divorce, the marriage must be annulled, which was why Rafe's father couldn't inherit the throne. The final stipulation was that the only suitable matches for a single heir to the throne were members of other royal families or the European nobility.

But since Rafe had yet to assume the throne, and this was still a new, untested document, there might still be room to maneuver. Or at least that was what Rafe hoped.

Rafe walked into the boardroom to find Gabe already there.

"I've been trying to get in touch with you all morning," Gabe said.

"Sorry. I had to turn the phone off. I needed time to think," Rafe said.

"Well, I'm the one that the family elected to

talk to you. Juan Carlos has been on the phone with the prime minister and the court advisors. They are insistent that we have a scandal-free transition back to the monarchy."

Rafe shoved his hands deep into his pockets and strove for the calm he'd always had when dealing with delicate business situations. And this was the most delicate merger of his entire life. He had to keep calm and not lose his temper.

"Thanks."

"Thanks. That's it? You're losing control of the situation and that's not like you," Gabe said.

"You think I don't know that? Emily is still trying to figure out if marrying me is a good idea. She's got morning sickness and looks more vulnerable every time I see her. The entire family desperately wants me to make this right and for once, Gabe, I truly have no idea how I'm going to do it."

Gabe clapped his hand on Rafe's shoulder. "You always make things work. I've seen you pull off deals that everyone else thought were lost."

Rafe nodded. He wished it were that easy. But from the first, this entire situation had too much emotion in it. There was Tia Isabella and her emotional plea for them to consider the offer from the Alma government to return to the throne. His father's bitter disappointment that he couldn't be the next king and his determination that his eldest son and namesake would be. All of it reeked of emotion, not common sense.

His chest felt tight and for once he needed that legendary coolness he was known for.

The rest of his family trickled in. Juan Carlos led the way. His expression read loud and clear: Rafe needed to act like a monarch and not a jet-setter.

Bella gave him a sad sort of smile as she came in. And his father's glare was icy to say the least. Gabe was sort of in Rafe's corner but he knew his brother didn't want to have to give up his lifestyle if Rafe abdicated.

Right now, he knew that was the only way for them to get him out of the picture.

After his family, the Alma delegation filed in. They had their lawyer and PR agent with them and quickly sat down on one side of the big walnut boardroom table.

His family settled in on the other side and Rafe took his customary seat at the head of the table.

"Rafael, has the girl agreed to marry you?" his father asked without preamble.

"We're not even sure he can marry her without the approval of this board," one of the members of the Alma delegation said.

"I think he should be allowed to marry. Look at the surge of popularity in the British monarchy after William and Kate tied the knot," Bella said with a wink at Rafe.

He gave his little sister a smile.

"A royal wedding would be grand. But we need to settle the subject of her being a commoner first."

"Did she say yes?" his father asked again. "If she's accepted then there is nothing more for this committee to consider. He's a Montoro and she's carrying an heir. The heir to the throne. I think that if he's engaged before the coronation that should be good enough for your council."

It was the first time Rafe could remember his father being on his side. Rafe was grateful to have his family's support for once in this situation.

"We can all appreciate that, Uncle Rafael," Juan Carlos said. "But Rafe has already let our family down and not just with the baby scandal. He's been very cavalier toward royal protocol and taking over the throne."

All of the voices at the table rose as everyone kept arguing their points until Rafe stood up and walked out of the room. He needed to come back to them when he'd made his decision and no sooner. Because they were going to keep fighting and tearing into each other, and in the end they'd tear him and Emily apart if he let them.

Emily wandered through the sculpture garden, admiring the eclectic collection. Famous sculptures stood next to pieces by unknown artists that reflected the Montoro taste.

As much as she'd enjoyed the few days she'd spent in Miami with Rafe, she was ready to go back to Key West. She'd be happy to grab her baseball bat and get rid of the reporters who'd been hanging around Key West hoping for a glimpse of her and then go back to normal.

She'd heard that life changed when a woman got pregnant, but this was more than she could deal with. She wanted things to work out for her and Rafe. For his family to just let her continue to try to figure out if marriage was a good idea or not.

"Emily?"

"Over here," she said, standing up from the bench where she'd been sitting and walking up the path toward Rafe's voice.

One look at his face and the turmoil of his expression and her heart sank. There was no way she could keep doing this to herself or to him. She knew in her heart that she would always love him, but she wasn't going to move to Alma. It hadn't taken more than a night in Miami to remind her how much she loved living in Key West.

"What'd they say?"

"They are still arguing about everything."

"Like what?"

"Whether I can I marry you, whether a royal wedding would be the PR coup of the year, whether I'm an embarrassment," he said.

"You're not an embarrassment," she said, taking a deep breath.

"My cousin Juan Carlos would disagree with you on that score. But none of that matters. I know I promised you time to make a decision but I do need your answer now, Red. Will you marry me? Be my partner on the throne in Alma?"

She bit her lower lip. Hesitating as she warred between what she knew was right for Rafe and what she'd started to believe she could have for herself. But he'd nailed it when he said they weren't sure he could marry her. She wouldn't be the reason he was ostracized from his family. She wouldn't be the reason he had to give up being king.

Her stomach roiled and she was afraid she was going to be sick again, but then realized it was nerves, not morning sickness. She took another deep breath.

Rafe cursed and gave her a hard look. "Seriously?"

"I can't marry you," she said. "While I'm sure that Alma is a lovely place, I can't imagine living there."

"It is lovely. You can have your own bar and do whatever you like once you are there."

"We both know that's not true. And I can't ask you to choose between me and the throne. I won't be the reason you aren't king, and there is a very real possibility of that happening. You'd resent me."

He shoved his hands in his hair and turned away from her.

She knew she'd made the right choice, but it hurt way more than she expected. "I know you'll support our child, but I'll be okay raising him or her on my own. I think I'll be good at that."

"I bet you do," he said, turning back around to face her. "No one there to interfere with any of your decisions."

"Don't get like that with me, Rafe. You know this is the only smart decision."

He stalked over to her and she realized he was truly mad at her. She'd done the noble thing. She was sacrificing her love and her dream of a family for him.

"I only know that you've hesitated from the moment you learned about our baby to involve me in your life. You keep pushing me away. I have given you space and tried to let you have the time you needed to see that we should be together. I know I seem angry. Hell, I am angry, but I really feel like you are making a mistake."

"And I know that you are. There is no world where you and I get to be together and raise this baby as we want to. I don't want our child to be raised with a bunch of rules on how to behave. You know that would happen. And I'm not good at conforming to them myself. It would be a constant headache."

"You're not going to change your mind, are you?"

"No."

"Fine. Go ahead and leave. You're good at being on your own. You said your mother let you be independent, but it's more likely that you pushed her away so you'd feel nice and safe with only yourself to be concerned over."

His words were mean and cut her to the core.

"You're just a spoiled man who can't handle the fact that he's not going to get his way in all things. That's what this is about. Not me or the baby, but you and your pride. They said you can't have me and the throne so you're trying to shove that down their throats. And to what end?" she demanded.

"Spoiled? You wrote the book on that, Red. I think you're describing yourself and not me. Normal couples, the ones you're always going on about, trust each other, depend on each other. And have each other's backs. They don't give themselves halfway to a relationship to try to keep from getting hurt the way you do. You don't care about anything or anyone other than yourself."

"Well, if that's how you feel I'm surprised you asked me to marry you."

"As you said, I just wanted to have it all. Make you mine for some ulterior motive. Never because I cared about you or wanted a family of my own."

She was too angry to listen as she stormed past him out of the sculpture garden and out of his life. But later she'd remember his words and cry.

Because at the end of the day, all she really wanted was to have a family with him.

Thirteen

Rafe watched Emily go and he was so angry that he didn't even contemplate going after her. Instead he thought sarcastically that at least his family would be happy. They wouldn't have to worry about him marrying a commoner any more.

But he needed time to calm down before he walked back into the boardroom, or he had the feeling he'd say something he regretted. He'd always been the one who was in control. Calm when he needed to be. Decisive. A man of action.

But then Emily stormed into his life and no

matter what decisions he made he still couldn't achieve the results he needed. He remembered how he'd felt on the boat in Key West when he'd looked over at Emily and realized he loved her. He'd been so focused on everything else that the love part seemed to have gotten lost.

His mom had told him when she left to never compromise with himself, because once that happened true happiness would never be his own. As a young adult he'd taken that to mean that he should live by his moral compass and not make business deals that were underhanded. But since meeting Emily he had the feeling that his mom had meant that sometimes making the right decision in society's eyes would be the wrong choice for the person he was.

He stood up and walked slowly back to the boardroom. He opened the door to find everyone still sitting around the table, but they were no longer all talking at once. Rafe knew that they had settled something while he'd been gone and he realized as king his choices were never going to be his own. He was always going to have to compromise and go to the committee before he could do anything.

"Good, you're back," Juan Carlos said.

"I am. What have you all decided?" Rafe asked as he walked to the head of the table and took his seat. "I think you should know that Emily and I will not be marrying."

"See, this just underscores my point," one of the officials from Alma said. "He can't control his personal life. He's a PR liability."

PR liability? He'd always played by the rules. He had a double degree in business management and geology—because of Montoro Enterprises' interests in oil—and he'd always known that without a good understanding of where they got their product he wouldn't be able to lead the company.

He'd worked hard for his family to build up the company so that there was no fear that this generation or the ones that followed would ever want for anything, and this was the thanks he got.

"A liability?" he asked. "Do you all feel this way?"

Juan Carlos nodded; Bella looked down at her fingers; his father just tightened his jaw. Gabe wouldn't make eye contact with him. Screw them. But he knew he was angry in general. He'd tried to please everyone—his family, the Alma delegation, Emily—and ended up not doing a good job of it for anyone.

He stood up and walked out of the boardroom and straight to his office. Jose was waiting there as always. "What do you need, sir?"

"I need to get to Key West. I'm afraid the chopper might not be a good option," Rafe said. He didn't want to take the company helicopter in case his services were no longer needed as CEO. "Can you have my car brought around?"

"Right away."

"Jose?"

"Yes, sir?"

"You've been a great assistant," Rafe said. "I'm not sure what is going to be happening at Montoro Enterprises. Please know that I will always have room for you on my staff wherever I am."

"Yes, sir."

Jose didn't ask any further questions and Rafe was grateful. He really didn't know how to explain anything other than that.

There was a knock on the door and he looked up to see Gabriel standing there. "Damn, I've never seen a man say so much with just a look."

Rafe shook his head as he finished gathering personal effects from his desk.

"There wasn't really anything else to say. I mean when your entire family thinks you've let them down, that's a horrible place to be."

Gabriel came farther into the room and leaned his hip against the desk. "You haven't let me down. I've never seen you so…alive as you've been in the last few weeks. I think that's because of Emily. If you can have her and be happy, you should go for it. That is what you're doing, right?"

"Yes," Rafe said. It had felt wrong to just let her walk away and now that he knew there really was no pleasing everyone, he was going to take care of himself and Emily first. He loved her and he was determined to convince her of it.

"Are you abdicating?"

"I am."

Gabriel cursed.

"I can't be king of Alma when my heart is here. I guess it never felt right to me being a monarch. I'm not aristocrat material."

"I'm sure as hell not either, but I think this means I'm going to have to clean up my act."

"I probably didn't make things any easier for you," Rafe admitted. "But you are a good man, Gabriel. I think you will make a very good king."

"Truly?"

"Yes. Better than me."

"No, I know you're lying. I'm going to pretend you're not. But I'm happy you have found someone."

"Don't be happy yet. She's stubborn and ticked off. I think it's going to take me a while to make her come around."

Gabe smiled at him. "I'm confident you're just the man to do that."

Rafe was, too.

He wished Gabe luck with his royal predicament and left Miami without talking to anyone else. Traffic wasn't too heavy in the midafternoon, but the drive was a long one and left Rafe time to think.

Deciding he wanted Emily was all well and good, but he knew he had his work cut out convincing her that she still wanted him.

Emily arrived in Key West just in time to shower and get dressed for work. It was a typical day in late June. There were too many tourists in town and she knew that she was cranky.

She started her shift with attitude. The first kid who presented her with a fake ID got it confiscated, then had a stern lecture from her before she had him escorted out of the bar.

The waitress and other bartender were all giving her a wide berth, which suited her. She didn't want to talk. She didn't want to think.

She simply wanted to forget everything that happened today, get through her shift and then get home.

Harry had looked at her once or twice and made as if he was going to come over and talk to her, but she shut him down with one hand in the air that told him she wasn't ready to talk. Tonight she had no idea whether she would ever be ready to talk about Rafe and the baby or anything.

Tonight all she needed to worry about was mixing drinks and keeping the tourists happy. She didn't even have to worry about reporters sniffing around anymore. Cara had told her this afternoon that another suspicious reporter had shown his face over at the coffee shop one more time. Cara and a few other locals had explained that he wasn't welcome in Key West anymore and told him to get the hell out of town.

It made Emily feel really good to know that these people had her back. She was home. This was where she and her child would live the rest of their lives together.

They would be fine. She knew that they would. It didn't matter that her heart was breaking right now. And that someday she might have to answer uncomfortable questions about where her baby's father was.

For tonight she was doing what she was good at. Rafe had accused her of being too self-sufficient and now she knew she couldn't deny it. She did get her guard up and isolate herself when things got uncomfortable.

Even when faced with love. But there was no way she was going to be the reason Rafael Montoro IV didn't become king of Alma. His great-grandfather Rafael I had been king when the family fled. She knew how important it was to the people of Alma and to the Montoros that Rafe sit on the throne.

Another kid came up to the bar and she gave him a hard stare. He looked as though he was eighteen if he was a day. "Kid, think twice before you place your order."

"What are you talking about, honey? I need a tube of LandShark for that table over there."

"Let's see your ID," she said, ready to rip him a new one.

But he pulled out his real ID and it showed he was nineteen. Off by two years. "I can't serve you beer, Alfred."

"It's for my dad and his buddies," Alfred said. "Dad, you're going to have to come over here."

Alfred's dad came over and got the beers and the rest of the night settled into a routine. This was going to be her life.

This was what she'd chosen. She could have been with Rafe wherever he was…but she'd chosen the safety of the only home she'd ever known over him. Not because she loved Key West so much but because it was safer to love a place than a man.

Key West wasn't going to leave her.

Rafe could.

"Why don't you take a break?" Harry said. "I've got some conch fritters on my desk and a nice fruit salad."

It was really a nice gesture from Harry. His way of saying that he was there for her. She walked over to him and gave him a hug. He hugged her back.

"You okay, kiddo?"

"I screwed up."

"Want to talk about it?"

She shook her head. "I think I'll start crying and maybe never stop."

"Go eat your dinner. That will make you feel better."

She went into Harry's office and found not only dinner waiting but Rafe.

Her breath caught and her heart felt as if it skipped a beat. She wanted to believe he was here for her, but what man would give up a throne for a woman like her?

"What are you doing here?" she asked. So afraid of his answer but she had to know.

"I abdicated."

"Oh, Rafe. Are you sure?"

"Very," he said, getting up and coming over to her. "I can't rule a country when my heart is somewhere else."

"Your heart?" This was more than she'd hoped

for. She had dreamed that he'd come for her but she'd never let herself believe it. She wasn't the kind of woman who a man like Rafe would give up everything for.

Yet she knew now that she was. She could see it in his hazel eyes and his wide grin. Only love made a person grin like that. She knew because she was grinning the same way.

"I love you, Red. I've never met another person who completes me the way you do. I know that sounds cheesy, but I'm new to this kind of thing."

She shook her head. "You can't abdicate. I don't want to be the reason you gave up the throne—"

"You aren't the only reason I abdicated, Em. My time in Alma was constraining. I didn't like having to follow all the rules or answer to a committee. That's not my way. I want to focus on you and our child. And I can't rule without you by my side. Plus, it wasn't really a choice when it came down to picking between you and Alma. You were miles ahead."

"Really?" she asked. "Miles?"

"Yes," he said, getting down on one knee in front of her. "Will you marry me?"

She got down on her knees in front of him and wrapped her arms around him. "I love you so much. I'm sorry for all the mean things I said today."

"Me, too," he said. "I think I knew even as you walked out that I was never going to be king of Alma. I didn't want it, especially given the way I needed you. So are you going to be Mrs. Rafael Montoro IV?"

"Yes."

He took the ring box from his pocket and put it on her finger.

"You should know that there is some question as to whether I will remain CEO of Montoro Enterprises...I might buy you that restaurant you were talking about after all."

"We can see about that. Am I dreaming this? Are you really here?"

"I am."

She still couldn't believe it. She was just so

happy to have Rafe in her arms and to know that he was going to be hers. She put her hands on his jaw and kissed him with all the love she'd been afraid to admit she felt for him. He held her close and whispered softly that he was never letting her go again.

There was a knock on the door and Rafe got to his feet, lifting her up, too. "You better eat your dinner."

She went over to the desk and sat down to her meal while Rafe opened the door. It was Harry. The two men exchanged a look before Harry smiled at her.

"Everything better now?" he asked.

She nodded. "I'm engaged."

Harry let out a whoop. "Drinks on the house. And you can take the rest of the night off."

Fourteen

The moon shone brightly down, warming them as Rafe led her toward the hammock in her backyard. The grass path under her feet was soft.

He stopped, turned her around and drew her into his arms from behind. His head rested on her shoulder and his big hands spanned her waist. She stood still, feeling the heat of his body against hers.

They fit perfectly together, which was something she'd rarely experienced in real life before Rafe. There was something about him that made everything sweeter. But this was a dream.

She found it hard to believe that she'd found a man she could trust with her heart and soul. But he was that man. She could just let go of everything and enjoy it. But a part of her was afraid to.

He turned her in his arms and she let him. He kept his hands at her waist and when she was facing him she was struck again by how he was quite a bit taller than she was. He gave her a half smile before he leaned in closer.

"You have a very tempting mouth," he said.

"I don't… Thank you?"

He gave a small laugh. "You are very welcome. It was one of the first things I noticed about you when you told me to wait in line at the bar. But I knew that you wanted something more from me."

"What?"

"You seemed to be begging me to kiss you," he said.

"Perhaps I was," she admitted.

His mouth was firm on hers as he took his time kissing her. He rubbed his lips back and forth over hers lightly until her mouth parted and she felt the humid warmth of his exhalation. He tasted so…delicious, she thought. She wanted more and opened her mouth wider to invite him closer.

She thrust her tongue into his mouth. He closed his teeth carefully over her tongue and sucked on her. She shivered and went up on her tiptoes to get closer to him.

His taste was addicting and she wanted more. Yes, she thought, she wanted much more of him, not just his kisses.

She put her hands on his shoulders and then higher on his close-cropped hair and rubbed her hands over his skull. He was hers now. Something that she could finally admit she'd wanted from the moment they met.

For a moment she felt a niggling doubt… There was something she should remember, but he tasted so good that she didn't want to think. She just wanted to experience him.

His hands moved over her shoulders, his fingers tracing a delicate pattern over the globes of her breasts. He moved them back and forth until the very tip of his finger dipped beneath the material of her top and reached lower, brushing over the edge of her nipple.

Exquisite shivers racked her body as his finger continued to move over her. He found the zipper at the left side of her top and slowly lowered it. Once it was fully down and the material fell away to the ground, he took her wrists in his hands and stepped back.

She was proud of her body and the changes that pregnancy had wrought in it. She could tell he was, too. His gaze started at the top of her head and moved down her neck and chest to her nipped-in waist.

He wrapped his hands around her waist and drew her to him, lifting her. "Wrap your legs around me."

She did and was immediately surrounded by him. With his hands on her butt and his mouth on her breasts, he sucked her gently, nibbling at her nipples as he massaged her backside. When he took her nipple into his mouth she felt everything inside her tighten and her center grow moist.

Then she felt as if she was falling and soon found herself lying on the hammock while he knelt over her. His mouth…she couldn't even think. She could only feel the sensations that were washing over her as he continued to focus on her breasts.

One of his heavy thighs parted her legs and then he was between them. She felt the ridge of his erection rubbing against her pleasure center and she shifted against him to increase the sensation.

She wanted to touch him, had to hold him to her as his mouth moved from her breast down her sternum and to her belly button. He looked up at her and for a moment when their eyes met there was something almost reverent in his eyes.

"My fiancée," he said. "Finally you and the baby are officially mine."

"Yes, we are."

He lowered his head and nibbled at the skin of her belly, his tongue tracing the indentation of her belly button. Each time he dipped his tongue into her it felt as if her clit tingled. She shifted her hips to rub against him and he answered her with a thrust of his own hips.

His mouth moved lower on her, his hands moving to the waistband of her jeans and undoing the button and then slowly lowering the zipper. She felt the warmth of his breath on her lower belly and then the edge of his tongue as he traced the skin revealed by the open zipper.

The feel of his five o'clock shadow against her was soft and smooth. She moaned a little, afraid to say his name and wake from this dream where he was hers. She thought she'd learned everything she needed to about Rafe, but it seemed there was still more for her to experience.

"Lift your hips," he said.

She planted her feet on the hammock and did as he asked. She felt him draw her jeans over her hips and down her thighs. She was left wearing the tiny black thong she'd put on this morning.

He palmed her through the panties and she squirmed on the hammock. She wanted more.

He gave it to her. He placed his hand on her most intimate flesh and then his mouth as he drew her underwear down by pulling with his teeth. His hands kept moving over her stomach and thighs until she was completely naked and bare underneath him. Then he leaned back on his knees and just stared down at her.

"You are exquisite," he said.

His voice was low and husky and made her blood flow heavier in her veins. Everything about this man seemed to make her hotter and hornier than she'd ever been before.

"It's you," she said in a raspy voice. "You are the one who is making me…"

"I am making you," he said. "And I'm not going to be happy until you come harder than you ever have before."

She shuddered at the impact of his words. He spoke against her skin so that she felt them all the way through her body.

"This is the one thing I should have done when you came to my penthouse in South Beach."

"Sex? Um, we did that."

"I should have taken you to bed and kept you there until you agreed to never leave me."

He parted her with the thumb and forefinger of his left hand and she felt the air against her most intimate flesh, followed by the brush of his tongue. It was so soft and wet, and she squirmed wanting—no, needing—more from him.

He scraped his teeth over her and she almost came right then, but he lifted his head and smiled up at her. By this time she knew her lover well enough to know that he liked to draw out the experience.

She gripped his shoulders as he teased her with his mouth and then tunneled her fingers through his hair, holding him closer to her as she lifted her hips. He moaned against her and the sound tickled her clit and sent chills racing through her body.

He traced the opening of her body with his other hand, those large deft fingers making her squirm against him. Her breasts felt full and her nipples were tight as he pushed just the tip of his finger inside her.

The first ripples of her orgasm started to pulse through her, but he pulled back, lifting his head and moving down her body and nibbling at the flesh of her legs. She was aching for him. Needed more of what he had been giving her.

"Rafe…"

"Yes?" he asked, lightly stroking her lower belly and then moving both hands to her breasts and cupping them.

"I need more."

"You will get it," he said.

"Now."

He shook his head. "That's not the way to get what you want."

She was shivering with the need to come. She had played these kinds of games before, but her head wasn't in it. She just wanted his big body moving over hers. She wanted him inside her. She reached between their bodies and stroked him through his pants, and then slowly lowered the tab of his zipper. But he caught her wrist and drew her hand up above her head.

"That's not what I had in mind," he said.

"But you are what I want."

"Good," he said, lowering his body over hers so the soft fabric of his shirt brushed her breasts and stomach before she felt the masculine hardness of his muscles underneath. Then his thigh was between her legs, moving slowly against her engorged flesh, and she wanted to scream as everything in her tightened just a little bit more.

But it wasn't enough. She writhed against him but he just slowed his touch so that the sensations were even more intense than before. He shifted again and she felt the warmth of his breath against her mound. She opened her eyes to look down at him and this time she knew she saw something different. But she couldn't process it because his mouth was on her.

Each sweep of his tongue against her clit drove her higher and higher as everything in her body tightened, waiting for the touch that would push her over the edge. She shifted her legs around his head, felt the brush of his silky smooth hair against her inner thighs, felt his finger at the opening of her body once again and then the delicate biting of his teeth against her pleasure bud as he plunged that finger deep inside her. She screamed his name as his mouth moved over her.

Her hips jerked forward and her nipples tightened. She felt the moisture between her legs and his finger pushing hard against her G-spot. She was shivering and her entire body was convulsing, but he didn't lift his head. He kept sucking on her and driving her harder and harder until she came again, screaming with her orgasm as stars danced behind her eyelids.

She reached down to claw at his shoulders as pleasure rolled over her. It was more than she could process and she had to close her eyes again. She reached for Rafe, needing some sort of comfort after that storm of pleasure.

He pulled her into his arms and rocked her back and forth. "Now I feel that we are engaged.

That you and I are going to be okay no matter what else happens in the world."

She shivered at his words and knew that she'd found the one man she'd never realized she'd been searching for. A man who could be her partner and respect her independence. The kind of man who'd be a good father and build a family with her.

"I've been meaning to ask you something," she said.

"What is it?"

"What did you want to be as a little boy? I never got to ask you," she said. She wondered about the man he'd become. Would his dreams have been to be a sports star or business tycoon? Well, he'd become that. Surely, he hadn't wanted to be king.

"I wanted to be your man," he said.

She punched him the shoulder. "Stop making fun."

"I didn't know that you would be the woman, Emily, but I always wanted a family of my own.

The chance to have someone who was always by my side."

"Well, you've got that," she said, kissing him.

* * * * *